Camp Club Girls

McKenzie's

MONTANA
MYSTERY

Camp Club Girls

McKenzie's

MONTANA
MYSTERY

Shari Barr

BARBOUR
PUBLISHING

Editorial assistance by Jeanette Littleton.

ISBN 978-1-60260-269-4

Published by Barbour Publishing, Inc., P.O. Box 719, Uhrichsville, Ohio 44683, www.barbourbooks.com

Our mission is to publish and distribute inspirational products offering exceptional value and biblical encouragement to the masses.

Member of the
Evangelical Christian
Publishers Association

Printed in the United States of America.

Dickinson Press, Inc., Grand Rapids, MI; Print Code D10002179; February 2010

CHAT ROOM TERMS:

2 – too, to

4 – for

B – be

BFF – best friends forever

GF – girlfriend

G2G – got to go

Kewl – cool

LOL – laugh out loud

LTNC – long time no see

RU – are you

Sum – some

Thx – thanks

TTFN – ta ta for now

TTYL – talk to you later

U – you

WTG – way to go

Y – why

A Surprise for McKenzie!

Aaaaaahhhh!

McKenzie screamed and clutched the reins with sweaty palms. She tugged firmly, trying to control her horse.

Please, God, help me, she prayed as Sahara bolted down the arena.

McKenzie's heart pounded and her auburn hair whipped behind her.

Something's wrong! she thought.

She leaned forward and pulled the reins with all her strength. The tightness she usually felt in the reins was missing. She had no control over her horse! Sahara raced straight toward the barrel in the middle of the arena.

"McKenzie!" a voice screamed from the sidelines. "Hold on."

The reins slipped between her fingers. McKenzie started to slide from the saddle. She grasped the saddle horn, but Sahara's galloping bounced her up and down until she could hold on no longer.

McKenzie hit the ground with a thud as thundering hooves barely missed her. She laid with her face on the ground. Sahara raced by and finally slowed to a trot.

"McKenzie! Are you okay?" A pair of cowboy boots appeared in front of her face.

Rolling over, McKenzie pushed herself into a sitting position. She coughed from the dust Sahara had stirred up and looked into the eyes of Emma Wilson, her riding instructor. "I—I don't know yet," she stammered as she stretched her legs.

She felt a strong hand support the back of her head. Turning, she saw Emma's hired hand, Derek, holding up two fingers. "How many?" he asked.

"Four," McKenzie answered.

Emma and Derek stared at her. No one said anything for a minute.

"But two fingers are bent over," she added.

After a second, Derek's face broke into a grin. He unbuckled her riding helmet and slipped it off her head.

"She's okay," a familiar voice announced. The girl with a fringe of black bangs fluttering on her olive skin popped a red gummy worm into her mouth.

"Bailey! What are you doing here?" McKenzie screeched as the girl approached her. "Hey, can I have one of those?"

"Yep, she's definitely okay," Bailey said as she dangled a green and orange worm in front of McKenzie.

McKenzie grabbed the worm and pulled her legs forward, trying to stand up. But Emma placed a firm hand on her shoulder. "Not so fast. Sit for a minute."

"What happened anyway?" McKenzie watched as her horse sauntered back across the arena and nuzzled her face. "I had no control over Sahara. I just couldn't hold on."

Derek reached his hand out to the chocolate brown mare. "Here's the problem," he said as his fingers touched a dangling strap. "Her bridle is broken."

McKenzie tried again to stand. Emma and Derek each put a hand beneath her arms and helped her to her feet. Feeling slightly light-headed, she stepped forward and grabbed Bailey in a tight hug.

"So, how did you get here?" McKenzie asked.

"When you told me you were coming to Sunshine Stables to train for the rodeo and help with Kids' Camp, I convinced Mom and Dad to let me fly out with Uncle Troy on a business trip. He rented a car and drove me out from the airport. He didn't have time to stick around, so he's gone already."

"Why didn't you tell me you were coming?" McKenzie asked.

"Well, I signed up for the camp, since I'm not that

good on horses. When Miss Wilson found out we were friends, she invited me to stay here, but she wanted to surprise you. Then after camp, she's going to train both of us for the rodeo." Bailey's dark eyes flashed.

"Oh, Emma, this is the best surprise ever!" McKenzie turned to her instructor.

"Think of it as a thank-you for coming to Kids' Camp on such short notice," Emma said with a smile. "I didn't expect so many kids to sign up. You'll be a big help with the younger ones. But, let's get you up to the house to sit for a minute. If you can walk, that is."

"I'm fine," McKenzie assured Emma as she brushed dirt from her face with the sleeve of her T-shirt. "I'd better take care of Sahara first, though."

"I'll do that," Derek said as he grabbed Sahara's halter. "I'll take her to the stable and find her a new bridle. You go on to the house."

Emma and the girls walked to the large, white farmhouse. A sign reading SUNSHINE STABLES stood in the front yard. Several sheds and a huge red barn stood beyond the house. The riding arena was next to a matching red stable. A dozen or so horses grazed in the lush, green pasture.

McKenzie sighed with contentment. She had met Bailey at Camp Discovery, where they had shared a cabin with four other campers. The six girls, or the Camp Club Girls, as they called themselves, had become fast friends by solving a mystery together. Though they all lived in different parts of the country, they had kept in touch and gone on to solve another mystery together. Bailey was the youngest of the group at nine years old, four years younger than McKenzie.

The girls stepped onto the huge porch that wrapped around the house. They dropped onto the porch swing while Emma slipped inside. Emma quickly returned with cold drinks.

"Emma, this is so perfect." McKenzie reached out to pet Buckeye, Emma's brown and white terrier. "This will be so fun having Bailey here. Now, we can work on barrel racing together."

"Don't forget you have to save time for the Junior Miss Rodeo Queen contest, too," Emma said as she ran her fingers through her short blond hair.

McKenzie groaned. She wasn't sure she wanted to compete in the contest. Emma had competed when she was younger and had told McKenzie's mom what a wonderful experience it had been. Now, Mom had talked McKenzie into competing. McKenzie didn't like the thought of wearing fancy riding clothes for the contest. And she especially dreaded the thought of standing on

11

stage in front of hundreds of people.

McKenzie got slightly nervous in riding competitions, but just thinking about the queen contest made her want to throw up.

"Are your parents coming for the rodeo and the queen contest?" Bailey scratched Buckeye's ears.

"Yes, they'll be here," McKenzie answered, sipping her lemonade. "My family doesn't live too far away. I usually come over here and train a couple of days a week. But now that I'm helping with Kids' Camp, I get to stay here until the rodeo next week. I'll have a lot of extra time to train."

After the girls finished their lemonade, Emma asked McKenzie to show Bailey their bedroom. The girls stepped inside the front door where Bailey had left her bags. She grabbed her pink and green striped pillow and tucked it under her arm along with a monster-sized black-and-white panda. McKenzie grabbed the two bags and led the way upstairs to their bedroom. A set of bunk beds stood against one wall.

McKenzie turned to her friend. "I knew you were hoping to visit, but I didn't think you'd be able to come."

"I didn't either." Bailey dropped her pillow and panda on the floor. "When Uncle Troy found out about his trip, Mom and Dad decided at the last minute that I could come along."

"We'll have a blast." McKenzie pointed to Bailey's bags. "Do you have cowboy boots in there somewhere? And you might want to change into jeans so we can go horseback riding as soon as Derek finds a new bridle for Sahara."

Bailey changed her clothes. Then the girls headed back downstairs and went outside with Emma.

"I'll help you saddle your horses," Emma said as she led the way across the yard. "Bailey, you can ride the Shetland pony, Applejack. Then you two can go for a ride while I work. How does that sound?"

"Great," McKenzie said. "When do we need to be back for chores?"

"About an hour or so," Emma said as they walked through the stable to Applejack's stall.

First Emma helped saddle the horse for Bailey, while McKenzie put the bridle on. Emma grabbed a riding helmet for the younger girl and led Applejack out of the stable.

Derek met them at the doorway holding Sahara, who was fitted with a new bridle. Derek was Emma's newest stable hand. He had only been working at Sunshine Stables for two months. Even though Derek was an adult, he reminded McKenzie of her eight-year-old brother, Evan. Both were always full of mischief.

"You look better than you did awhile ago," Derek told McKenzie. "You're not even limping."

"Nope. I told you I was fine." She patted Sahara's neck.

"McKenzie, why don't you introduce your friend to Derek? I didn't have a chance to do that when you were taking your wild ride," Emma teased.

McKenzie pulled Bailey to her side. "Bailey Chang, meet Derek McGrady. Bailey lives in Peoria, Illinois."

"Nice to meet you, Bailey. You ready to hop on Applejack? He's ready for you." He grabbed the horse's reins and opened the gate.

McKenzie followed with Sahara. She placed her boot in the stirrup and swung herself up onto the saddle. Then with ease, Bailey hopped onto Applejack's back.

"Your mom said you've done quite a bit of riding, Bailey. Is that right?" Emma asked as she closed the gate behind them.

"Yes. But I'm not as good as McKenzie." Bailey swept her long bangs away from her forehead and slipped on her helmet. "I've done some racing at county fairs but never a rodeo."

"You're a lot younger than she is. You have plenty of time to improve." Emma smiled at Bailey.

"Is it okay if we ride to Old Towne?" McKenzie put her helmet on and fastened the chinstrap.

"Sure. You have your cell phone with you, right?" Emma asked. "After you look around for a while, head back for chores. Both of you can help with Diamond Girl when she comes in from pasture."

Diamond Girl was Sunshine Stable's most famous horse. She was Emma's prize horse and a rodeo winner. For the last three years, Emma had ridden Diamond Girl in the barrel-racing competition, and each year Emma brought home the first-place trophy. McKenzie couldn't wait to show Diamond Girl to Bailey.

Eager for a ride, the girls waved to Emma and Derek and headed for the dirt track behind the house. A warm summer breeze rustled the pine trees lining the trail.

"What is Old Towne?" Bailey asked as her horse plodded beside McKenzie's.

"It's a bunch of Old West buildings. There's an old-time Main Street with a general store, post office, and stuff like that. But it's more like a ghost town now. It belongs to Sunshine Stables and is open during June, July, and the first week of August. It's closed now for the season. But we can still go look around." McKenzie shielded her eyes against the sun and peered into the distance.

Pointing her finger, she continued, "See that old wooden windmill way out there? That's Old Towne."

"It looks kind of creepy." Bailey wrinkled her nose.

"You know, there is a spooky story about Old Towne." McKenzie flicked her reins at Sahara who had stopped to munch some grass. "A long time ago, a mysterious rider was seen riding out there at dusk. Some people say it was a ghost rider."

Bailey looked quizzically at McKenzie. "Is that for real?"

McKenzie chuckled. "That's what they say."

"Has anybody seen the ghost rider lately?" Bailey nudged Applejack forward.

"I haven't heard anything about it. Emma said the ghost rider story started years before she bought Sunshine Stables. She says someone just made it up to get visitors to come to Old Towne. It worked. Old Towne used to rake in the money. People paid to ride horses from the stables, hoping to see the ghost rider."

"That's spooky. A fun kind of spooky, that is," Bailey said as she leaned over and scratched Applejack's neck.

"Well, let's go check the place out. I've never been here after it was closed for the season."

McKenzie nudged Sahara with her heels. The girls galloped down the trail. The horses' hooves stirred up little puffs of dust.

"Here we are," McKenzie said as she arrived at the top of a small hill. She halted Sahara and waited for Bailey to catch up.

"Wow! This is neater than I thought it would be!" Bailey exclaimed, her eyes wide.

The girls continued down the trail leading to Main Street. Old storefronts lined both sides of the dirt street. A weathered school building and a church were nestled on a grassy lawn at the edge of town, away from the other buildings.

"Let's tie our horses at the hitching post and look around." McKenzie hung her helmet on the post and fluffed her sweaty curls.

After tying both horses, the girls stepped on the wooden sidewalk. Bailey ran ahead, her boots thumping loudly on the wood. She stopped and peered through a streaked windowpane. A tall red and white barber pole stood beside it.

"I can just imagine a cowboy sitting in there getting his hair cut," Bailey said with a giggle.

"Yeah, and then he could head across the street to the general store for a piece of beef jerky and a new pair of chaps." McKenzie stuck her thumbs in her belt loops and walked bow-legged across the street.

Bailey laughed and raced to catch up with McKenzie. She stopped suddenly in the middle of the street and looked at the dusty ground. "Hey, did cowboys eat candy bars?"

McKenzie picked up the wrapper and shoved it in

her pocket. "Maybe the ghost likes the candy. Whooo-ooooh!" McKenzie wailed eerily.

The girls headed to the general store and peered through the window. McKenzie pointed out different items in the darkness. They saw old wooden rakes, hand plows, and row after row of tin cans on the shelves. A headless mannequin wore a long, lacy white dress, and a pair of men's bib overalls hung from a hanger.

Both girls jumped when McKenzie's cell phone rang. She pulled the phone from her pocket, answered, and listened to the caller for a minute. Then she quickly said, "Okay. Bye," and flipped the phone shut.

"That was Emma," she said. "She wants us to hurry home. Diamond Girl is missing!"

Missing!

As the girls rode back to the house, McKenzie prayed that they'd find Diamond Girl. Not only was she a treasured racehorse, but Emma also planned to use her as a therapy horse once her racing days were over. McKenzie had helped at a horse therapy center the year before. She'd watched angry kids calm down as they worked with, rode, and took care of the horses. She'd also seen the horses have a good affect on disabled people and adults who were dealing with problems. Diamond Girl's calm nature made her perfect to work with disabled or troubled kids and adults.

Since Diamond Girl was already older than most racehorses, Emma had said that this might be Diamond Girl's last year to race in the rodeo.

God just has to keep her safe, McKenzie thought. *Too many people depend on her.*

When the girls arrived back at Sunshine Stables, McKenzie hoped to see Diamond Girl safely in her stall.

But she only saw three stable hands cleaning out the stables, refilling the stalls with fresh hay.

"Has anybody found Diamond Girl yet?" McKenzie called as she hopped off Sahara's back.

Ian, a kindly middle-aged man, shooed a fly away from his dark brown face as he walked to the girls. "No sign of her yet. Emma and Derek are still searching. Looks like somebody left a gate open. She's been out to pasture all afternoon, so there's no telling how far she's gone by now."

McKenzie couldn't believe someone would leave a gate open. All stable hands knew to close the gates behind them. She met Bailey's worried gaze. "Can we help look for her?" McKenzie asked.

"Emma wanted you girls to take care of your horses and put them up for the night," Ian said as he stuck his pitchfork into a hay bale.

McKenzie held the reins as Ian removed Sahara's heavy saddle. Then Ian removed Applejack's saddle while McKenzie and Bailey removed the horses' bridles.

After McKenzie turned the horses into the corral, she turned to Bailey. "We'll leave them out here while we clean their stalls. Then we'll bring them in for the night."

McKenzie and Bailey each grabbed a pitchfork and pitched dirty hay and manure into wheelbarrows.

McKenzie heard the stable hands quietly talking to each other. Everyone seemed anxious, McKenzie thought. She guessed the workers were eager to finish chores and help look for Diamond Girl.

When the girls had cleaned the stalls, they covered the floor with fresh, sweet-smelling hay and filled the water troughs and feed bunks. McKenzie rested for a moment, leaning on her pitchfork as she wiped her sweaty forehead with a T-shirt sleeve.

She looked at her young friend, struggling to keep up. McKenzie knew Bailey had asthma, so she got winded easily. Fortunately, the hay didn't seem to be bothering Bailey at the moment. "Let's take a break. I'll grab a couple of sodas."

McKenzie went to a fridge in a small room at one end of the stable and grabbed two cans of strawberry pop.

After handing Bailey a pop, McKenzie popped the top of her can and enjoyed the cold drink trickling down her throat. She listened to the soft whinnies of the horses and smelled the musty mix of hay and horses. A horse in the next stall snorted.

"We'd better bring Sahara and Applejack in now." McKenzie swallowed the last of her drink. "It's almost their suppertime."

McKenzie and Bailey soon had the halters back on

the horses. After giving the horses a quick rinse with a hose, the girls led them into the stable.

The stable hands were feeding the last of Emma's horses and by the time McKenzie and Bailey finished with their horses, the chores were all done. McKenzie felt as though she hadn't helped much. She hoped Emma wouldn't regret asking her to stay and help. The two younger girls couldn't work nearly as hard as Emma's older employees.

Ian approached the girls as they put their pitchforks and wheelbarrows away. He lifted his worn cowboy hat and scratched his black curly hair. He looked at the girls as if he wanted to say something.

"Emma's been gone a long time. Haven't they found Diamond Girl yet?" McKenzie asked, again offering a silent prayer.

Ian hesitated and then answered. "Emma called awhile ago. She found no hoof prints at the open gate. Emma doesn't think Diamond Girl wandered off. Every other gate in the pasture is locked. She thinks the mare was stolen."

McKenzie felt her heart pounding. "Stolen! Who would steal Diamond Girl?"

Ian shrugged as the girls followed him out of the stable. "Emma and Derek are on their way back, and the sheriff is on his way out to talk to the stable hands. Emma said you girls should go to the house and get something to eat. It could be a long night."

Though she wanted to wait for the sheriff, McKenzie agreed they should have supper. She led Bailey across the yard and up the back steps of the house.

"Do you think somebody really stole Diamond Girl?" Bailey asked as she kicked off her cowboy boots.

"Ian seems to think so." McKenzie splashed cold water on her face from the sink in the mud room. "I've been praying that she's safe ever since I heard she was missing."

"Yeah, me, too," Bailey said as both girls headed into the kitchen. "I've never even seen Diamond Girl. What's she like?"

McKenzie took packages of sliced ham and cheese from the fridge. "She is the prettiest horse you ever saw. Shiny black with a white diamond shape on her forehead, and she's the fastest runner around here. When Emma rides her in the rodeo, no other horse stands a chance of winning."

After pouring two glasses of milk and making sandwiches, the girls carried their plates to the front porch. As McKenzie said the blessing for the meal, Buckeye sat at their feet to beg bread crusts.

While they ate, the girls saw Emma and Derek ride in from the pasture on their four-wheelers. The sheriff's dirty white pickup truck pulled in the driveway, and he headed toward the stables. McKenzie wished she could hear what the sheriff was saying, but she knew it wasn't any of her business.

The sun was low in the western sky when the sheriff drove off and the stable hands left. Emma approached the house and sank into a wooden chair on the porch with a deep sigh.

"What a day!" Emma said as she stretched her legs and closed her eyes. "I can't believe everything that's happened."

"Did someone really steal Diamond Girl?" McKenzie asked as she tucked her legs beneath her on the porch swing.

For a second she thought Emma wasn't going to answer. When Buckeye laid his head on Emma's lap, she opened her eyes. "It looks that way. I had hoped and prayed it wasn't true, but we see no signs that Diamond Girl ran off."

Emma looked so sad that McKenzie wanted to cheer her up, but she didn't know what to say or do. She knew Emma would be devastated without Diamond Girl.

"Do you think the sheriff can find her before the

rodeo?" McKenzie asked. She didn't want to think about Diamond Girl not being able to compete, but she couldn't help it.

"I certainly hope so," Emma said. "But I just hope that wherever she is, she is okay. Competing in the rodeo isn't that important as long as I get Diamond Girl back safe and sound."

McKenzie nodded. Surely no one would hurt a horse as gentle as Diamond Girl. She couldn't imagine anyone being that mean.

"Can we help do something?" McKenzie asked softly. "We can get things set up for Kids' Camp tomorrow."

"I could fix you a sandwich." Bailey swatted a mosquito on her arm.

"You girls are great." Emma smiled as she rose from her chair. "Everything is pretty much ready for the kids tomorrow, but I'll take you up on that sandwich, Bailey."

As the sun dipped below the horizon, they all stepped inside. While Emma washed up, Bailey and McKenzie fixed her a light supper.

"Would you mind if we use your computer for a few minutes, Emma? We usually go to a chat room about this time each night." McKenzie poured a glass of iced tea and set it on the table for Emma. "I can't wait to tell the other girls that Bailey is here."

"Of course," Emma said. "Make yourselves at home. If I'm not using the computer, feel free to e-mail or chat or whatever."

As the girls headed to Emma's office, the phone rang. "Hi, Maggie," McKenzie heard Emma say. McKenzie could tell Emma was talking with Maggie Preston, the owner of a neighboring stable, Cedar Creek Ranch. "You won't believe what's going on around here." Emma informed Maggie of Diamond Girl's disappearance.

The girls continued down the hall and into the office. After pulling an extra chair up to the desk, McKenzie logged on to the Camp Club Girls chat room. She found their four friends already chatting.

Alexis: *Hey, Mckenzie, where've U been?*

Alexis wrote from her home in Sacramento, California. Sydney was online in Washington, D.C. Kate lived in Philadelphia and Elizabeth in Texas. Though the girls lived in different parts of the country, they tried to chat online frequently. And when they were on a case, like they'd been with the mystery at Camp Discovery and Sydney's adventure in D.C., they also texted and used other forms of communication to solve mysteries together.

Sydney: *Everybody's here but Bailey.*

McKenzie typed as fast as she could: *R U ready for*

this? She's here with me. Big surprise! She's staying 2 train for the rodeo with me.

Kate: *WTG Bailey. How kewl! Tell McKenzie 2 teach U sum of her trix. She really knows how 2 ride.*

After the girls had chatted for a few minutes, Bailey reached over and typed a quick message: *Sunshine Stable's prize horse has been stolen. The sheriff was here. Hope 2 find her.*

Alexis: *Y would someone steal her?*

McKenzie: *Dunno. Guess sheriff will figure that out.*

A message popped up on the screen from Elizabeth, who at fourteen was the oldest: *McKenzie and Bailey, maybe God brought U 2 together this summer 4 a reason. Maybe He wants U 2 figure out what happened 2 the horse.*

McKenzie and Bailey looked at each other. Elizabeth always seemed to remember to turn to God for the right answers. McKenzie often wished she were more like Elizabeth. She often forgot that with God, everything happens for a reason.

McKenzie: *Maybe U R right, Elizabeth. Maybe there's more work 2 do here than train 4 rodeo.*

Sydney: *Hey, another mystery 2 solve. Wish I was there.*

McKenzie: *Time 2 go. TTYL.*

While McKenzie logged off, she glanced out the

window. A sliver of moon shone in the sky. Pale streaks of violet and pink were all that remained of the sunset. She shoved the extra chair back against the wall and heard Emma's voice in the kitchen. McKenzie could tell she was still on the phone with Maggie.

"Did you see a light out there?" Bailey asked as she peered out the window.

McKenzie returned her gaze to the window. The trees and shrubs were shadowy shapes in the darkness. "I don't see anything except some lightning bugs."

Bailey looked again out the window. "I thought I saw a light clear out there in the pasture." She pointed. "But I don't see it now."

The girls watched awhile longer, but when the light didn't reappear, McKenzie stepped away from the window and turned off the desk light. As they walked into the kitchen, Emma was just hanging up the phone.

"News sure travels fast." Emma placed dirty dishes in the dishwasher. "Maggie, over at Cedar Creek, saw the sheriff go by and wondered if something was wrong. I asked her to watch for any unusual activity around here. I'd hate to think horse thieves are in the area."

"Do you think the thieves will come back?" Bailey asked.

"Oh, I didn't mean to frighten you, Bailey." Emma

placed an arm around the younger girl's shoulders. "The sheriff suggested we keep a close eye on things. Maggie volunteered to have one of her men patrol the area at night, and I agreed. I can't ask my team of workers to work a night shift when Kids' Camp is starting tomorrow."

McKenzie knew Diamond Girl's disappearance was serious, but knowing the sheriff had asked Emma and the neighbors to patrol their ranches worried her even more. McKenzie had never heard of horse thieves in this area, and the thought scared her. What if the thieves did come back?

"I've scared you both," Emma said as she slung her other arm around McKenzie's shoulder. "I'm sorry this had to happen when you were here, but with God's help, everything will work out. We have to trust Him on this." Emma yawned. "It's been a long day. Why don't you two head on upstairs. I'll clean up down here."

Both girls flung their arms around Emma's neck and told her good-night. McKenzie was tired and ready for bed. She knew the next day would be a busy one. When the campers left in the afternoon, she and Bailey needed to practice for the rodeo. In less than two weeks, the competition would begin.

As McKenzie showered, she thought of Sahara and all

the rodeo events she needed to work on. Not only that, but she'd also be responsible to help Bailey. By the time she had slipped into her pajamas, she felt better about Diamond Girl's disappearance. Surely the sheriff would have some news soon.

When she stepped into the bedroom, she saw Bailey leaning on the windowsill. Bailey turned to McKenzie, and her voice trembled. "I just saw another flash of light in the pasture. Something is out there!"

The Clue at the Creek

McKenzie's heart quickened. She dashed to the window. "Where did you see the light?"

Bailey pointed toward a cluster of trees at the far edge of the pasture. "It was there a minute ago," she said. "It really was."

"I believe you." McKenzie peered into the darkness. "Maybe it's some of Maggie's workers patrolling the area."

Bailey sighed and moved away from the window. "I just hope it's not the horse thieves returning."

"They wouldn't hang around. They know people will watch for them now. I'm sure they're long gone." McKenzie picked up her brush from the dresser and yanked it through her thick wet hair.

"Do you think we can help find Diamond Girl?" Bailey asked as she unpacked her bags into a couple of dresser drawers.

McKenzie climbed onto the top bunk and dangled her legs over the side of the bed. She had wanted to offer to look for the horse, but she figured Emma would want the sheriff to handle it. But after Elizabeth had mentioned it in the chat room, and now Bailey, it seemed like a good idea.

"Maybe so," McKenzie said. "If the sheriff doesn't find out something by morning, let's ask Emma if we can investigate."

"How will we have time to do everything? We're at Kids' Camp every morning. Then, in the afternoons, we'll train for the rodeo," Bailey said as she pulled out a bag filled with bottles of nail polish of every color.

"We'll find time," McKenzie said. "We won't practice all afternoon. Then we'll have evenings, too. And, since Kids' Camp is only for a few days, we'll have more free time after that."

"But you'll have to get ready for the Junior Miss Rodeo Queen contest sometime, too," Bailey said with a frown. "I wish I could be in the contest."

McKenzie wished she hadn't agreed to compete. It was the last thing she wanted to do this summer, and Bailey wanted nothing more than to be in it. It didn't seem fair that Bailey couldn't enter when she wanted to so badly.

"I wish you could, too," McKenzie stretched on her stomach and hung her head over the bunk. Her hair hung down as she looked at Bailey. "But the Junior Miss Rodeo Queen contestants have to live in Montana. I wish I could trade places with you."

Bailey's eyes grew wide. "You're kidding! How come you're entering it then?"

McKenzie shrugged her shoulders, as well as she could while hanging upside down. "Because Mom wants me to."

"Did you tell her you don't want to be in it?" Bailey asked as she alternated painting her toenails orange, yellow, and purple.

McKenzie swung herself back up on the bed. She stretched her leg and pulled the chain for the ceiling fan with her toes. "No. I didn't have the nerve. She thinks I wanted to enter. She'd be disappointed if I backed out now."

"I don't believe you don't want to be a rodeo queen." Bailey shook her head as she waved her feet around to dry the polish. "I would love to be queen almost as much as I'd love to find Diamond Girl."

McKenzie wished she had the enthusiasm for the contest that Bailey had. All she really cared about now was finding the stolen horse. Winning a contest didn't seem to matter much.

She shut off the light and thought about the horse

thief. Maybe she should pray for him instead of just Diamond Girl. She asked God to be with the person who had taken the horse. Whoever had stolen her must have a horrible problem to do something like that. As she asked God to help her forgive that person, she drifted off to sleep, dreaming of Diamond Girl's safe return.

●—●—●

At breakfast the next morning, Emma told the girls she had heard nothing new from the sheriff about Diamond Girl. He had spoken with all the neighbors, but no one had seen anything out of the ordinary.

"We're pretty good at solving mysteries. Would it be all right if we try to figure out what happened?" McKenzie asked through a bite of cinnamon roll.

"I don't see why not," Emma said. "Maybe you can find a clue the sheriff overlooked. The campers leave at 2:00. After you practice with Sahara, you can do what you want."

Shortly before nine o'clock, the kids began arriving for camp. Emma gathered everyone under a large, shady oak tree in the front yard. The more experienced riders, including Bailey, would train with Emma. McKenzie would help Derek and Ian with the beginning and average riders.

First the campers helped feed and groom their

horses. Then the younger kids learned to mount and ride. As McKenzie worked, she watched Emma helping Bailey and the other riders learn how to barrel ride.

Barrel riding was McKenzie's favorite rodeo event. Three barrels were set up in the arena in the shape of a large triangle. Each contestant raced to the first barrel and made as tight a turn as possible around it before moving on to the second and third barrels. After turning around the last barrel, the rider raced her horse across the finish line. The rider with the fastest time would be the winner.

Bailey handled the horse well. Soon she had Applejack galloping around the barrels.

Applejack had been trained in the rodeo event, so he could almost run the course without a rider. He was a gentle horse who ran only as fast as Bailey urged him.

The day flew by and at two o'clock, the campers went home. Applejack had worked most of the morning, so Bailey led him to his stall to rest. Since McKenzie hadn't ridden all morning, she brought Sahara to the paddock.

Sahara stood still as McKenzie mounted her. McKenzie combed the horse's thick brown mane with her fingers, feeling her warm, velvety back rippling beneath her touch. Sahara twitched her head and neighed, telling McKenzie she was eager to run.

"I think Sahara's ready," Emma hollered across the arena as she leaned against the white fencing. "Take her for a few laps. Then we'll work on the barrels."

McKenzie flicked the reins and Sahara leaped forward. McKenzie let her body move with the motion of the horse. Together they flew around the arena with McKenzie's hair flying behind her like a streamer. Round and round they sailed.

After warming up for a few minutes, McKenzie slowed the horse to a walk, but Sahara wasn't ready to rest. She wanted to run.

Emma signaled McKenzie to begin, so she dug her heels into Sahara's side. The horse leaped forward as they flew toward the first barrel. McKenzie pulled on the reins, guiding Sahara in a tight circle around it.

Then she raced toward the second barrel. After circling the third barrel, McKenzie squeezed Sahara's side with her calves, urging her to go faster. As they crossed the finish line, Emma clicked the stopwatch.

"Great run, McKenzie," Emma called out. "You beat your last time by half a second."

McKenzie rode over to the fence where Emma and Bailey waited. Her face flushed with pride. She knew she had to work hard if she wanted to win at the rodeo. "Do you think I stand a chance of winning?" McKenzie asked.

"Sure," Emma said as she patted Sahara's back. "But you have a lot of tough competition. Last year's winner will be racing against you. If you push yourself, you can easily make the top three. But remember, McKenzie, doing your best is what matters the most. God doesn't expect any more than that, and neither does anyone else."

McKenzie knew that, but it was hard to believe sometimes. She knew God wanted her to do her best, but by winning she would know she had done that. If she didn't even place in the top three, she would always feel as if she hadn't tried hard enough.

This would be her third year to compete in barrel racing at the rodeo, and she had finished in the bottom half each time. This year she was determined to get at least second or third place.

"Let's try it a few more times," Emma said.

Again, McKenzie and Sahara flew through the course. The sun beat down on them, and McKenzie felt the sweat trickling down her back. She tried to make as tight of turns as she could around the barrels. Every split second counted in barrel racing. When Emma shouted that it was quitting time, both horse and rider were relieved.

"You had some great runs, McKenzie," Emma said as she approached Sahara.

Bailey had said nothing while McKenzie practiced.

When McKenzie glanced at her, she turned away. Was Bailey upset about something? She seemed almost sad. McKenzie wondered if she was homesick.

"I need to call Sheriff Danby. Hopefully he will have some news about Diamond Girl," Emma said as she glanced at her watch. "You can start your investigation if you want, but why don't you get some cold drinks while the horses rest?"

McKenzie gave Sahara a quick rinse to cool her off, and then the girls grabbed two bottles of water from the supply room. Fifteen minutes later, they rode into the pasture behind Sunshine Stables.

"You really did good on Applejack this morning, Bailey." McKenzie adjusted her riding helmet.

"Not really," Bailey said with a frown. "You're lots better than I am. You'll win for sure."

So that's what's bothering her, McKenzie thought. She remembered how she had felt when she had first begun barrel racing. She had thought everyone was better than she was.

"You were great, Bailey," McKenzie said cheerfully. "I've been racing for years. This is your first time. You're better than I was when I started."

Bailey shrugged her shoulders. "You're just saying that. There's still no way I'll win anything."

McKenzie pulled on the reins to stop her horse. "It doesn't matter if you win. You're probably the youngest person in our division. You've only been riding horses for a little while, and you're already competing in a rodeo. How many kids get to do that? You were great. I mean it."

Bailey smiled but didn't answer as she reached over and scratched Applejack's neck. The horse whinnied softly as he plodded beside McKenzie and Sahara.

"Let's head to the gate that was hanging open." McKenzie led the way across the pasture. "Emma and Derek said Diamond Girl didn't go through it because there were no hoof prints, but maybe we can find a clue there, anyway."

McKenzie knew the gate that had been left open was on the far side of Sunshine Stable's land. Soon McKenzie turned to Bailey and pointed to a gate about a hundred yards away. "There's the gate we're looking for."

As the girls approached the gate, McKenzie slid off Sahara's back. She looped the reins around a fence post and patted the horse. Sahara leaned across the fence and began munching the tall, green grass on the other side. McKenzie turned to the gate, which opened onto a dirt road.

"Emma and Derek are right. The ground is soft and no tracks are here. The grass hasn't been trampled and there aren't any tire tracks, either. So, no one parked on the road and hauled her off in a trailer." McKenzie searched the ground looking for clues.

"So, who opened the gate? And why?" Bailey dismounted Applejack and walked to McKenzie.

"I don't know. It's really weird. The gate has a solid latch, so someone had to open it on purpose." McKenzie leaned against the fence, staring into space. "It's almost like someone wanted us to think Diamond Girl escaped through the gate."

"Hey, maybe that's it." Bailey's dark eyes sparkled. "The thief could have parked on the road and walked over to open the gate. That's why there are no hoof prints or tire tracks."

"I think we're on to something," McKenzie said with excitement. "The thief could have stolen Diamond Girl from another part of the pasture. Then he could have opened this gate to throw everyone off."

"So what do we do now?" Bailey asked with a frown.

"Well, the thief must have taken her through a gate. Right? So, we need to check the other gates to the pasture." McKenzie pulled Sahara's reins from the fence post and mounted her.

"How many gates are there?" Bailey asked as she pulled herself onto Applejack's saddle.

McKenzie thought for a minute. "Three other ones,

I think. And this pasture is big, so it'll take awhile to get around to all of them."

As they rode, McKenzie tried to think of people who might want to steal Diamond Girl, but she couldn't imagine anyone doing something that awful. Almost everyone in the rodeo business had heard about the prize-winning horse, so anyone might have done it. The horse would bring a large sum of money if the thief sold her. Surely the thief wasn't someone she knew.

McKenzie couldn't stand the thought of never seeing Diamond Girl again, so she knew how Emma must feel. Her instructor would be devastated if they didn't find Diamond Girl.

McKenzie led the way across the valley behind Sunshine Stables. As they approached the next gate, she quickly checked the ground beyond it.

"No trailer has backed up here, that's for sure," McKenzie said with a sigh. "She must have been stolen through one of the last two gates. Let's check them out."

But the girls didn't find any evidence at either of the other gates. McKenzie was not only disappointed, she was also confused. How could Diamond Girl have been stolen? No tracks of any kind disturbed the ground beyond the gates.

"I don't get it," Bailey remarked. "She couldn't have

disappeared into thin air."

McKenzie sat in the saddle. "The only other opening into the pasture is next to the stable," she told Bailey. "Surely Diamond Girl didn't leave that way. Surely a thief couldn't just walk out the front gate with her without anyone seeing them."

"This just doesn't make sense!" Bailey said.

McKenzie wiped the sweat from her forehead with the back of her hand. "These horses need a drink. Let's head to the stream, and then we'll head back. I'm hot."

The girls rode slower now that the late afternoon sun was beating down on them. At the top of the rise, McKenzie stopped and gazed at the stream below them. After leading the horses to the creek bank, the girls dismounted to let them drink. McKenzie pulled off her boots and socks. She rolled up her jeans and waded into the stream, letting the cool water bubble around her ankles as it tumbled over rocks from high in the mountains.

"Come on in," McKenzie called to Bailey. "The water's great."

As the horses drank, the girls splashed in the foaming water. Within minutes they were laughing and playfully shoving each other.

"We'd better head back," McKenzie said through her

laughter. "Emma will wonder what happened to us."

Bailey walked up the bank, with water streaming down her legs. Her black hair was plastered to her head. Water trickled down her face onto her red tank top. Little globs of mud stuck to her like an explosion in a chocolate bar factory.

"You look like a river rat," McKenzie teased as she wiped her face with her T-shirt hem.

Bailey stuck her tongue out at her friend. "I can't look as bad as you, can I?" she kidded McKenzie.

"All right. That does it. You're getting dunked." McKenzie laughed as she lunged toward the younger girl, grabbing her arm.

Bailey twisted out of her grasp and fell into the shallow creek. Even with Bailey on her knees, the water only reached the tops of her thighs. "Hey, look what I found," she said as she reached into the water. "An old horseshoe."

With water dripping from her elbows, she stood and handed it to McKenzie, who examined it.

"Bailey," McKenzie said as she scrutinized the horseshoe. "You're a genius! This isn't any old horseshoe. It's Diamond Girl's!"

CHAPTER 4

A Wild Ride!

"How do you know the horseshoe is Diamond Girl's?" Bailey asked as the girls walked up the grassy bank.

"Emma had custom horseshoes made for her. See the little diamond shapes on the arch." McKenzie traced her finger along the engravings. "But I guess it really doesn't mean anything. It just means she came down here to drink, and all the horses do that."

"I think we should consider this a clue," Bailey said. "Detectives should take every piece of evidence very seriously. She had to lose the shoe yesterday before she disappeared or someone would have noticed, right? We just need to figure out where she went from here."

"You've got a good point. Maybe she wandered out through a hole in the fence." McKenzie surveyed the barbed wire fence stretched across the shallow part of the creek, looking for a broken wire. But every wire was secured tightly.

"What about tracks?" Bailey asked. "Wouldn't it be

easy to track a horse with one missing shoe?"

McKenzie looked up with a grin. "Great idea, Bailey."

Both girls returned to the creek's edge, looking for tracks in the dirt.

"You mean, not so great," Bailey grumbled after a few minutes. "All the hoof prints around here have been washed away from our splashing."

McKenzie continued to look, searching for tracks farther up the creek. All the tracks seemed to come from horses with all four shoes in place. She sighed hopelessly. "I feel like we've overlooked a clue, but I don't know what else to do."

"Detectives take pictures of the crime scene to go over later. Maybe you could do that," Bailey suggested. "Your cell phone takes pictures, doesn't it?"

"Brilliant!" McKenzie said as she pulled her phone from her jeans pocket. "I hope it didn't get too wet."

She flipped open the phone. It seemed dry, so she quickly snapped pictures of the ground. She didn't really know what she hoped to find, but maybe they would see a clue they had missed when they reviewed the pictures later.

Applejack and Sahara had waded into the stream to cool off and waited patiently. After leading their horses up the bank, the girls slipped into their boots and headed for home. Though the sun was still hot, the breeze felt almost cool against their wet clothes.

After arriving back at the stables, the girls removed the horses' tack and led them to the corral and the watering trough.

"Let's find Derek or Emma and show them the horseshoe," McKenzie suggested.

They found Derek at the far end of the stables and showed him their find. They explained their theory to him.

"It's Diamond Girl's all right," Derek said. "I'm sure she went to the creek yesterday to drink, but that part of the creek has a lot of large rocks to catch a horse's shoe. I really don't think it's a clue to her disappearance. I'm sorry, girls."

McKenzie's face fell at Derek's remark. She had convinced herself that the horseshoe was the first real lead they had found. Now she was beginning to think it didn't mean a thing.

As Derek left with a wheelbarrow full of old hay and manure, the girls headed through the stable.

"I was hoping the horseshoe was a clue," McKenzie said with a sigh.

"Me, too," Bailey said dismally. "But maybe we'll find a real clue soon."

McKenzie suddenly stopped and peered into the

nearest stall. "Let me show you one of Emma's special horses. Her name is Krissy, and you'll like her. But first I need to get Derek to help."

The girls stood to the side as the stable hands hauled wheelbarrows of hay to the stalls. Nightly feeding and grooming had already begun. McKenzie would quickly show Krissy to Bailey, and then they would need to help with chores.

McKenzie hurried to the supply room and grabbed a handful of baby carrots from the fridge. She asked Derek to help with Krissy. Then she returned to Bailey's side.

McKenzie opened the stall door and stepped inside. An older black horse covered with white splotches lifted its head at the sound of the girls' voices.

Bailey gasped and flung her hands over her mouth while her dark eyes gleamed. After a few seconds she finally spoke, "An Appaloosa! This is my favorite breed of horse. I've always wanted one!"

McKenzie laughed as she stepped to Krissy's side and patted her back. "See the big white spots that look like snowflakes. They look like Christmas snow, so Emma named her Krissy, like Kris Kringle."

Bailey ran her hands through Krissy's mane. The horse tipped her head toward Bailey and whinnied. Krissy obviously loved the attention. The horse stood still as Bailey stroked her spotted back.

Soon Derek arrived carrying a stack of bright cardboard signs.

"Are you ready for the good part?" McKenzie asked as she untied Krissy's lead rope. "This horse is very talented."

McKenzie turned the horse around and held on to the rope. "We're ready if you are," she said to Derek.

He held up three cards and looked at the horse. "Okay, Krissy. How many signs am I holding? Count for me," Derek said.

Bailey looked skeptically at McKenzie. Then she turned her gaze back to Krissy. The horse lifted her head and nodded one, two, three times. Bailey's mouth fell open as she turned back to McKenzie.

"Did that horse just count?" Bailey asked with surprise.

"Yep, she sure did," McKenzie assured her as she offered Krissy a carrot.

"Do you want to try it?" Derek asked Bailey.

"Sure," Bailey said eagerly.

Derek handed Bailey the stack of cards, then grabbed a pitchfork and stepped into the next stall.

Bailey held up four cards. "Okay, Krissy. How many cards am I holding?"

The horse simply looked at Bailey, refusing to nod. Again, Bailey asked Krissy to count.

This time the words "one, two, three, four" came out of Krissy's mouth. Bailey jumped back, dropping the signs. For a minute she stood speechless, staring at the horse.

Finally McKenzie could control herself no longer. She burst out laughing and cried, "Derek, that's a mean trick to play on your new friend."

Derek's head popped over the top of the stall, and his laughter filled the stable. "Haven't you ever seen a talking horse before?" he said, though his mouth didn't move.

Bailey stared at him for a minute, then grabbed a handful of straw and threw it at him, laughing. "Are you a ventriloquist?"

He dodged the straw and turned back to Bailey. Again, his mouth didn't move as he spoke, "Only when I need to be."

"Wow, you are really good," Bailey exclaimed. "How do you do it? And how did you get the horse to count by nodding her head?"

Derek continued to scoop hay and manure. "I've been practicing ever since I was a kid. I performed in a few talent shows when I was younger. As for teaching Krissy to count, that's my little secret." He turned to McKenzie and winked.

Though McKenzie had tried to get Derek to tell her the secret, he wouldn't let her in on it. McKenzie turned to Krissy and secured her lead rope. After grabbing a brush from the ledge, she began stroking the horse's back. "I wish you could talk, Krissy. Then maybe you could tell us what happened to Diamond Girl."

No one answered for a few seconds. Derek leaned on his pitchfork and took off his cowboy hat. He pulled a bandana from his back jeans pocket and wiped the sweat from his face. "I know you girls are worried about that horse. But there's really not much anybody can do."

McKenzie grew worried at his words. Did he think no one would ever find Diamond Girl? Surely he didn't really believe that.

Bailey seemed to read McKenzie's mind. "Can't the sheriff find her?" The younger girl pulled a tube of watermelon lip balm from her pocket and ran it across her lips.

"He's called all the auction companies in the area, but no thief would try to sell a prize horse like Diamond Girl around here. She would be easily recognized. But some thieves know how to disguise a horse, so she could be sold anywhere. No one would ever find her." Derek shook his head dismally.

McKenzie stared at Derek. Surely God wouldn't let

Diamond Girl just disappear off the face of the earth. They just had to find her, and she would keep trying until they did.

McKenzie wanted to tell Derek and Bailey not to give up hope, but as soon as she opened her mouth, a figure at the end of the stables caught her eye. She turned as a woman approached them.

McKenzie recognized Maggie Preston—the neighbor Emma had been on the phone with the night before. She owned Cedar Creek Ranch, which was next to Sunshine Stables. McKenzie wondered how long Maggie had been standing there. Had the woman been listening to their conversation?

"Derek, I'm surprised to see you're still around here. I thought you'd be gone by now." The woman flicked a piece of straw off her red T-shirt. "Is Emma around? I need to talk to her."

Derek pushed the wheelbarrow to the next stall. "She ran into town to pick up a load of feed. Can I do anything for you?"

Maggie handed Derek a flyer. "Would you mind posting this somewhere so your riders can see it? I'm offering calf-roping sessions for teams who want to practice for the rodeo, and I only have two time slots left."

Derek took the flyer and looked it over as Maggie

continued. "I mainly wanted to ask her about Diamond Girl, though. I'm so worried that something awful might have happened to her. I came by to tell her I'll do anything I can to help. If she doesn't feel up to taking on all those kids this week, she can feel free to send them my way. After all, Emma owes me."

Without another word, she turned and marched out of the stable. Derek shook his head as he watched her leave.

"Why was she surprised to see you here, Derek? Are you leaving Sunshine Stables?" McKenzie asked.

"No. I'm not leaving. Not yet, anyway. But I would like to start my own stable some day, and I need to save a lot of money before I can do that," Derek said as he stepped back into a stall.

McKenzie hoped Derek wouldn't leave. She'd had so much fun since he had come to Sunshine Stables.

"What did she mean by saying Emma owes her?" McKenzie grabbed another pitchfork and began scooping old hay and manure from another stall.

"Several of Maggie's riding students dropped out and are going to Emma's Kids' Camp instead. I guess she's a little upset about that," Derek said.

McKenzie couldn't believe anyone could be angry with Emma. She was such a sweet person. McKenzie had often thought that if she had an older sister, she would want her to be like Emma. Could Maggie really be upset because she had lost a couple of her young riders to Kids' Camp? It was just a one-week program. McKenzie wondered if something else was bothering the woman. *Could Maggie know something about Diamond Girl?*

"Well, Emma would never take Maggie's riders on purpose." Bailey folded her arms across her chest as she defended her instructor.

Derek nodded. The three raked old hay out of the stalls in silence. After they had filled several wheelbarrows, Derek stood up and stretched.

"Emma wanted that lean-to off the barn cleaned today," he said. "Some old machinery is in there, but everything else can be thrown on the trailer to be hauled off. It shouldn't take long. Would you girls do that?"

"Sure," McKenzie agreed. She loved messing around in the hayloft of that old red barn. Emma's cat, Cheetah, often had a litter of kittens up there. Working in the barn sounded good.

On their way out of the stable, McKenzie stopped in the supply room for a pair of binoculars. From the hayloft in the barn, a person could see the countryside for miles. She thought Bailey might enjoy the view.

McKenzie led Bailey through a gate leading to the

back of the barn. She swung the door open and stepped inside, breathing the musty smell of old hay. Sunlight streamed through the cracks in the walls.

The barn was a large, tall building supported by heavy wooden beams. The hayloft stretched across one end of the barn and was piled with hay bales. An old wooden ladder stood at one side reaching to the floor of the loft.

McKenzie hung the binoculars around her neck by the leather strap and tugged on Bailey's arm. "Do you want to go up?" McKenzie asked as she headed toward the ladder.

Bailey stood at the foot of the ladder and peered up, frowning. "Oooh, I don't know about this," she said in a trembling voice. "It's awful high up."

"Oh, you'll love it once you get up there," McKenzie said, stepping onto the first rung. "I'll go first."

McKenzie continued climbing until she stepped onto the loft. She knelt and peered down over the edge. "Come on. It's really neat up here."

Bailey wrinkled her brow as she stared at McKenzie. "I don't like high places. I don't think I can do it."

"Sure you can. Step on the first rung and take it one step at a time, but don't look down. You'll do fine." McKenzie held out her arm toward Bailey.

Taking a deep breath, Bailey stepped on the ladder.

Climbing slowly, she finally reached the loft as McKenzie clutched her arm.

Bailey glanced around at the bales. "Wow, this really is cool," she said, brushing the dust from her hands.

"Come to this window." McKenzie scampered to a pile of bales and climbed almost to the top of the barn. She turned and leaned out the open window as the breeze brushed her cheeks. She could almost reach out and grab a branch in the treetop.

Bailey's hands trembled as she held the binoculars to her eyes. She gasped. "Hey, I can see the old windmill turning at Old Towne and the barber shop and. . .I see someone in the woods behind Old Towne."

McKenzie grasped the binoculars and peered into the distance. "I see it, too," she said as a flash of red moved slowly through the trees. But whoever it was disappeared quickly into the timber.

Bailey wrinkled up her nose and sneezed. "Ooh, it's dusty in here," she said as she covered her nose with her hand.

McKenzie knew that because of Bailey's asthma, sometimes hay and dust bothered her. "Why don't you go outside? I'll start carrying out those boxes."

Bailey frowned. "I have my inhaler. I can help."

McKenzie didn't want to take the risk of her friend

having an asthma attack. "I'll do it," she assured Bailey. "But see those two horses near the fence. Bring the brown mare, Molly, in here through that other gate. Grab a brush and give her a rubdown, and she'll love you forever."

The girls climbed down the ladder and headed outside, Bailey to get Molly and McKenzie to the lean-to.

As McKenzie's eyes adjusted to the darkness, she saw the shapes of old machinery at one end. Boxes and cans littered the other end. She grabbed a box filled with old leather straps and tack and loaded it onto the trailer parked outside the door. She carried box after box, and as she was finishing, something furry rubbed against her leg. She shrieked and jumped back.

After glancing nervously at her feet, she chuckled. "Cheetah, you scared me half to death." McKenzie bent over to pet the cat's soft fur.

As she stood up, she noticed several crates behind an old wooden horse cart. The crates were crammed into the corner, so she would have to move the cart to get to them. McKenzie grabbed the cart and rolled it outside.

"This is a great horse, McKenzie," Bailey called out as she brushed the mare's back. "She's as gentle as a bunny."

"I thought you'd like her. Her eyesight is going bad, but she can still run," McKenzie said as she headed back for the crates. They were heavier than they looked, so she rearranged the contents before she could lift them. She looked up as a shadow filled the doorway.

"Hey there, Buckeye. How are you doing, boy?" she asked as the dog trotted to her side.

Buckeye sat beside her, content to have his ears scratched.

Until he saw Cheetah.

With a leap and a yowl, he was on his feet. Cheetah's back arched. She hissed and spat before she sprang for the door with Buckeye close behind. Within seconds, McKenzie heard a frantic neigh and a piercing scream.

McKenzie raced to the door. As Molly lunged against the gate, the latch slipped, and the horse raced into the open pasture. McKenzie was surprised to see that Bailey had hitched the old horse cart to her.

McKenzie scanned the corral to find Bailey. She couldn't see her anywhere. But then she spotted Bailey, her black hair flying behind her as she clung to the sides of the old horse cart! It dangerously careened from side to side as the nearly blind horse ran uncontrollably! Bailey screamed again, hanging on for dear life!

The Stranger

"Bailey!" McKenzie screamed. "Hold on!"

She ran to the chestnut horse grazing nearby. Since she had no time to saddle the horse, she climbed the fence, and with a quick jump she was on his back. Clinging to his mane, McKenzie clucked and dug in her heels.

The horse leaped forward and McKenzie raced after Bailey and the runaway horse. She leaned forward until she was almost lying on the horse's neck, urging the horse to run faster. Soon she gained on the old brown mare. Bailey shrieked more, spurring Molly to go even faster.

The wind whipped McKenzie's hair and curls flew in her face, but she didn't let go. Her only choice was to get close enough to the mare to slide onto her back. McKenzie prayed that the mare would slow down. With the extra weight of the cart and Bailey, Molly finally showed signs of tiring. McKenzie urged her horse onward, slowly gaining on the mare.

When she was neck and neck with Bailey's mare, McKenzie called out in a soothing voice, "Hey there, Molly. It's okay. Easy, girl."

Soon the mare slowed. McKenzie glanced at Bailey still gripping the sides of the horse cart. The younger girl's eyes were wide with fear.

It's now or never, McKenzie thought as she inched closer to Molly. She leaned over to the mare and grabbed the halter. With all her strength, McKenzie pulled herself onto the mare's back.

McKenzie tugged on the reins to slow down the mare, talking softly to Molly until she slowed to a walk. With another tug on the reins, McKenzie finally brought the mare to a halt.

"You okay, Bailey?" McKenzie asked. Bailey still gripped the horse cart.

Bailey didn't answer for a moment; then she pushed her tangled black hair out of her face. "I think so," she whispered.

McKenzie leaned forward, feeling Molly pant beneath her. She couldn't believe she had just ridden bareback and jumped onto a moving horse! She was glad it was over and that Bailey was all right.

"Wow, that was some ride," McKenzie said after she caught her breath.

Bailey sat cross-legged and still in the cart. Her face was pale with little pink spots on both cheeks.

"You can get out now," McKenzie continued as she patted the mare. "This old girl's not going anywhere for a while."

"I don't think I can," Bailey mumbled. "My legs are scared stiff. They won't move."

McKenzie laughed. "You think you were scared? I can't pry my fingers off these reins."

Bailey pulled her legs from beneath her and stretched. "You were great, McKenzie. I can't believe you did that! It was just like in the movies!"

"Well, if that's Hollywood, I've had enough," McKenzie said as she sat up straight. "Hey, where did my horse go?"

The girls glanced around the pasture and spotted the horse about a hundred yards away.

McKenzie took a deep breath. "We'd better go round him up and head for home. I'm going to have a talk with Buckeye when I get back. No more scaring cats around the horses."

"I don't have to ride back here, do I?" Bailey asked from her seat in the horse cart.

"No way. You can ride Molly back. She should be okay now that there aren't any cats around." McKenzie hopped off and helped Bailey onto the mare's back. Her knees felt wobbly after her daring ride. She grabbed the reins and led the mare toward her horse.

The girls didn't speak as McKenzie walked beside Molly and Bailey. She glanced up at her young friend who was staring straight ahead, slouched in the saddle. McKenzie knew the runaway horse had frightened Bailey, but now that the incident was over, Bailey seemed more embarrassed than scared.

McKenzie knew that her younger friend was a talented rider, especially for someone with as little training as she'd had. But Bailey had little confidence in herself when she was around the older Camp Club Girls. McKenzie knew how important it was for Bailey to be a good horseback rider, but this incident sure wouldn't help matters.

As the girls approached McKenzie's chestnut horse, Bailey exclaimed, seemingly forgetting the runaway horse episode. "Hey, look. Someone else is out riding. His horse is gorgeous."

McKenzie looked across the fence, about fifty yards away, at a young man struggling with his horse. He was clearly frustrated with the animal, so he didn't notice the girls. But Bailey was right, the horse was beautiful.

McKenzie had never seen a horse like this one. She

looked like a brown American paint horse with large white splotches and stockings.

"Hey," McKenzie called out. "Do you need some help?"

The young man looked up, apparently surprised to see them, but he didn't answer. His horse bounded closer to the fence, snorting loudly. The man jerked on the reins, but the horse reared on her hind legs.

McKenzie stared in disbelief. He seemed to have no clue as to how to handle the animal. She felt sorry for the poor horse. The horse acted like she wanted to throw her rider.

No animal deserves to be treated like that! McKenzie thought angrily.

As McKenzie looked at the horse, she thought the horse looked familiar, but she knew if she'd seen a horse with that coloring before she'd remember it.

"I can help you calm your horse, if you'd like," McKenzie called out. "I've worked with horses quite a bit."

The young man glared at her and snapped, "I don't need your help. I've got it under control."

McKenzie winced. It was clear he didn't have things under control. He acted as if he'd never ridden a horse before.

"Your horse is beautiful. What's her name?" Bailey called, her eyes glistening.

"Would you two just leave?" he stammered in a raised voice, ignoring her question. "Can't you see you're scaring my horse?"

McKenzie looked sheepishly at Bailey. "I think we'd better go. Can you handle Molly by yourself? Then I'll ride my horse."

Bailey patted Molly affectionately. "Sure. We're friends now, aren't we Molly?"

McKenzie stepped up on the fence to mount her horse. The young man had gained some control of his horse. She clucked at her horse and headed back toward Sunshine Stables.

In the distance, she saw a rider on horseback racing toward them. As he drew nearer, she recognized Derek. Within minutes, he pulled up alongside them, holding his battered white cowboy hat against his chest.

"You two okay?" he asked breathlessly. "I heard screaming, and then I saw Molly flying across the pasture with Bailey in the cart. I was unloading feed, or I would have been here sooner."

Bailey looked down as a flush came over her cheeks. "I'm fine. I did a dumb thing, I guess."

Derek flashed a grin at Bailey but didn't scold her. Apparently, he figured out what had happened.

"Well, at least nobody was hurt. I don't think I even

want a ride that wild," he said as he jumped off his horse. "Why don't you take my horse, Bailey, and I'll take Molly and the cart."

Bailey gave Derek a relieved look and slid off Molly. "I like that idea."

After Derek helped Bailey onto the saddle of his horse, he turned to McKenzie. "Are you all right riding bareback?"

McKenzie assured him she would be fine. Then she asked, "Do you know that guy back there?"

Derek looked to where she was pointing. "I don't see anyone."

McKenzie looked back and sighed. Where could he have gone so quickly? "He was there a minute ago. He was riding a beautiful brown paint horse with white spots."

"And his horse wanted to throw him off," Bailey piped up.

Derek shrugged his shoulders. "I don't know anyone around here with a horse like that. Maybe one of the riders at Cedar Creek brought his own horse."

McKenzie hadn't thought of that, but Derek was probably right. The rider had been on Maggie's land, and he looked and acted like a beginning rider. McKenzie knew lots of adults who wanted to learn to ride and took lessons.

McKenzie and Bailey led the way back while Derek followed them with Molly and the cart. As they rode back, McKenzie mentioned the flyer Maggie had brought over earlier.

"I entered the calf-roping contest at the rodeo last year and it was a lot of fun. Would you want to be my partner? I would show you how to do it," McKenzie swatted at a mosquito perched on her arm.

"That sounds like fun, but how would we practice? Emma doesn't have calves," Bailey asked.

"Maybe we could sign up for one of Maggie's calf-roping sessions." McKenzie urged her horse as they approached the backside of the old barn. "What do you think?"

"I think it's a great idea," Bailey said. "I just hope Emma will let us."

Emma was waiting at the barn for the girls when they returned. "Thank God you two are all right," she said, giving each one a hug. "You had me worried for a minute."

They told Emma the whole story as they groomed, fed, and watered the horses. They asked their instructor if they could sign up for calf-roping sessions at Maggie's place.

Emma thought for a minute and then said, "I don't

see why not. I'll call her after supper. I'm starved. Let's go inside. We're finished here."

The girls fixed the toppings for a pizza while Emma made the crust. After placing the pizza in the oven, Emma went to call Maggie.

The girls slipped out to the front porch as the sun dipped low in the western sky. Soon it would disappear behind the nearby mountains.

McKenzie loved living near the mountains and had lived here all her life. With the mountains practically in her backyard, she could go skiing and snowboarding in the winter whenever she wanted. Sunshine Stables was in the valley about thirty miles from her home and had been a perfect place for her to train with Sahara.

Buckeye came up the steps, stopping to sniff a baby kitten. Cheetah hissed at him from her perch on the porch railing. Bailey scooped up her little orange kitten and dove onto the porch swing, cuddling the tiny bundle in her arms.

"Oh, no you don't, you big mean dog," she scolded playfully.

McKenzie called Buckeye to her side and scratched his ears. Soon he laid his head in her lap and closed his eyes, while McKenzie daydreamed about the rodeo. Every year she looked forward to competing, but this year it was hard to get excited. A part of her looked forward to it, but she felt almost guilty with Diamond Girl missing. If no one could find the horse, Emma couldn't enter the rodeo. McKenzie couldn't imagine the rodeo without Emma and Diamond Girl.

McKenzie jumped when Emma opened the screen door with a loud creak. A wonderful smell of sausage and seasonings floated out.

"Pizza's ready," Emma said. "I called Maggie, but she's already filled the last two time slots. She did say you could go over and watch the other teams practice, though. McKenzie knows how to rope, but it would help you, Bailey, to watch the event a few times."

"When can we go?" Bailey slid into a chair at the kitchen table.

"I told her Friday afternoon. Kids' Camp will be over, so that will give you more time. How does that sound?"

"Great," McKenzie said. "Then we'll have the other afternoons this week to work with our horses."

During supper the girls talked back and forth, but Emma said little.

"You miss Diamond Girl, don't you?" Bailey asked with her mouth full of pizza.

Emma looked up suddenly. "I guess I do," she said with a sigh. "I just hope she's okay."

"We're still working on the investigation," McKenzie said. "We're good at finding clues others miss."

Emma reached out and grabbed McKenzie's hand. "I think this is an investigation for the sheriff, but you can keep trying if you want. Don't forget the main part of this investigation is prayer, and we all need to remember that we have to accept God's will in all this. He wants us to learn from this, no matter what happens, okay?"

McKenzie knew Emma was speaking the truth. Her parents had always told McKenzie and her little brother that with God, everything happened for a reason. When bad things happened, it was to bring them closer to Him. God promised never to give them more than they could handle as long as they had faith.

Emma pulled away and changed the subject. "Oh, by the way, McKenzie. Your mom called and said your outfit for the Junior Miss Rodeo Queen contest came in. I picked it up at Boots and Buckles when I was in town." Emma disappeared into the dining room.

She returned a minute later holding an outfit on a hanger. Bailey gasped and her eyes widened as she stared at the pants and top.

McKenzie loved the outfit. In fact, it seemed prettier than when she and her mom had picked it out. The crisp black western style jeans looked perfect with the emerald green riding blouse, while dozens of matching green sequins on the cuffs and collar flickered in the light.

"You'll look gorgeous in this," Emma said as she touched a sparkling sequin. "You'll be the prettiest girl on the stage."

McKenzie said nothing. Usually she liked trying new things. But now heaviness settled in her stomach. If only she hadn't let her mom talk her into entering the rodeo pageant. She stared at the riding outfit. Emma had told her she would have a lot of fun, but McKenzie was seriously starting to doubt that. She knew she would only embarrass herself as well as her family if she got up there on stage.

She decided right then and there that she wasn't going to let that happen. Competing in a rodeo queen contest wasn't her thing. It was okay for Emma and okay for her mom, but there was absolutely no way she would wear that outfit. Not in the Junior Miss Rodeo Queen contest. Not ever! She'd figure some way out of it!

CHAPTER 6

The Ghost Rider Returns?

"What's the matter, McKenzie?" Emma asked. "Isn't this the outfit you and your mom picked out?"

McKenzie's mouth felt dry as a cotton ball. "Oh, it's the one we ordered, all right," she stammered as she placed her elbows on the table and cupped her chin.

Emma laid the outfit over the back of a kitchen chair. "Then what's wrong?" she asked with concern.

"She doesn't want to be in the contest," Bailey answered, then slapped her hand over her mouth. "Oops. I'm sorry, McKenzie. I didn't mean to tell."

Emma pulled out the chair next to McKenzie and sat down. "Is that right, McKenzie? Do you really not want to be in the contest?"

McKenzie folded her arms on the table and put down her head. "Yes," she mumbled. "I mean 'yes', then 'no.'"

Emma gently stroked McKenzie's hair as she asked softly, "But why? I thought you wanted to be in it."

McKenzie answered sullenly. "I don't want to get all

dressed up and stand in front of a bunch of people with judges staring at me. But I have to do it because Mom wants me to."

Emma stopped stroking McKenzie's hair for a second. Then she started in again. "Aah. I see. Does your mom know you don't want to be in it?"

"Nope," Bailey answered again with a sigh. She held the blouse up to her chest and checked the sleeves for length against her own arms. "She doesn't want to hurt her mom's feelings."

"Oh, McKenzie, you need to talk to her, if you feel that way. I'm sure she wouldn't want you to compete if she knew you really didn't want to." Emma patted McKenzie's arm. "But why don't you sleep on it and call her tomorrow. You know I was really nervous, too, the first time I competed. But I'm so glad I did. You might change your mind, too."

McKenzie looked up and thought about Emma's words. Her instructor might be right, but McKenzie wasn't ready to admit it just yet. It wouldn't hurt to wait one more day to call her mom. Besides, she didn't want to upset her mom this late in the evening.

McKenzie stood up and began clearing the table.

"Isn't it about time to chat with your camp friends? Why don't you see if anyone is online while I clean up the kitchen?" Emma gathered the remaining dishes and carried them to the sink.

The girls headed into the office. After logging on, they noticed their other four friends were already chatting.

Kate: *Where have U 2 been?*

Alexis: *Have U found the horse yet?*

McKenzie: *Still working on it. Not many clues yet. Tho we did find Diamond Girl's horseshoe in creek.*

Sydney: *Maybe DG disappeared from that spot.*

McKenzie: *We thot of that, but there was no gate and the fence across the creek had no holes.*

Elizabeth: *It's only been 2 days. Something will turn up. Remember Ecclesiastes 3:6 says, "a time to search and a time to give up." I think God wants U 2 search longer. Don't give up on DG yet.*

McKenzie knew the Bible verse Elizabeth was talking about. The scriptures talked about how there was "a time for every purpose under heaven." McKenzie knew that everything happens for a reason, but right now she couldn't imagine what that reason could be.

Elizabeth: *Hey, McKenzie, R U ready 2 B rodeo queen?*

McKenzie cringed. *I want 2 drop out. I'll get 2 nervous.*

Elizabeth: *U can't do that. U have 2 enter. U'll do great.*

Alexis: *Yeah. I would luv 2 B queen. U can't quit!*

After the Camp Club Girls chatted a few more

minutes, McKenzie agreed to seriously reconsider the queen contest. Maybe it wouldn't be so bad after all.

As she logged out of the chat room, she turned to Bailey. "I almost forgot the pictures I took with my cell phone. Let's put them on the computer and see if we find a clue."

McKenzie loaded the pictures onto the computer, magnifying each picture one at a time. With their heads together, the girls studied them, hoping to see something that looked out of place. McKenzie's eyes grew tired staring at the screen, and she was almost ready to give up when something caught her eye.

"Look." McKenzie touched her finger to the screen, pointing out a yellow object on the ground. "What is that?"

Bailey peered closer. "I can't tell. Is it a wrapper or something?"

"I'm not sure," McKenzie said. "It's too late to check it out now, but maybe we can go back to the creek tomorrow afternoon. Hopefully it's not paper and won't blow away."

After scanning the remaining pictures, the girls saw nothing else that looked unusual. McKenzie wondered what detectives looked for. She hoped she didn't miss a clue that was right in front of her eyes.

McKenzie stretched her arms above her head and yawned. "Let's be done for the night. Okay?"

McKenzie logged off the computer and stepped out of the office. When she saw the rodeo outfit draped over a chair, she felt a sudden urge to try it on. Maybe Emma and the Camp Club Girls were right. A spark of excitement began to form deep inside her.

Minutes later, the girls were in their room. Bailey flung herself onto her bunk, hiding her face in her pillow.

"Tell me when you're ready." Bailey's voice sounded muffled. "I don't want to look until I see the whole package."

McKenzie changed out of her clothes and slipped into the new black jeans and shimmering green blouse. She added her new black cowboy hat and boots, then finished off the outfit with a matching black belt with a large silver buckle.

"Ta-da!" McKenzie posed with one hand on her hips.

Bailey pulled her face from her pillow and gasped. Then her lip trembled as she stared at McKenzie.

"What's the matter?" McKenzie asked as she glanced down at her outfit. "Do I look stupid?"

Bailey turned away and said nothing. Without looking at McKenzie, she finally answered, "It's not fair."

McKenzie didn't understand. "What's not fair?"

"You don't even want to be queen and I do, but I can't because I don't live here." Bailey's voice cracked as she spoke.

For a minute, McKenzie didn't know what to say. Maybe she should drop out of the competition after all. The last thing she wanted to do was to hurt Bailey's feelings.

But as soon as the thought went through her mind, she knew she couldn't do that. She had already promised her mom, and after talking with the Camp Club Girls, she had decided to go ahead with the competition as planned.

Now that McKenzie knew Bailey's true feelings, she needed to figure out a way to include her younger friend.

McKenzie glanced in the mirror over the dresser at her shoulder-length auburn curls flowing beneath the cowboy hat and wondered how she should wear it for the contest—a low ponytail maybe, or she could just let it hang loose.

She frowned as she rubbed her cheeks, wishing she could simply rub away the sprinkling of freckles across her nose. With a sigh she turned to Bailey. "I might get through this queen thing after all, that is if you'll help me with my hair and makeup. Mom got me a kit and said I could wear a little, but only for the contest. But you're better at doing hair and makeup than I am. Would you help me with it?"

Bailey sniffed and turned around. Her eyes were red. "I guess I could do that. Everything has to look just right, you know. You can borrow my nail polish, too. It matches your top perfectly." Bailey tried to smile as she held out her neatly painted green fingernails.

The girls said little as they changed into their pajamas and slipped into their bunks. McKenzie heard a coyote howl outside and Buckeye barked an answer, but she was so tired the howling didn't bother her. Before she could finish her prayers, she had fallen asleep.

●—●—●

McKenzie didn't wake up until she smelled blueberry muffins baking the next morning. Within minutes, both girls were dressed and sitting at the kitchen table. McKenzie had just finished her third muffin when the first of the campers arrived for the day.

McKenzie and Bailey hurried outside to meet them as a woman in a van dropped off three kids. All of them were rowdier than usual.

"My older brother's girlfriend saw the ghost rider last night," one young boy exclaimed to his friend.

"Your brother's just making it up," another boy argued.

A girl who looked about Bailey's age said, "No sir. My

grandpa says the ghost rider is back. Several people saw him riding around last night. Kind of like a ghost—at dusk." The girl made a high-pitched eerie ghost sound.

McKenzie and Bailey exchanged glances.

Did several people really see the ghost rider? McKenzie wondered. She thought it was just a story someone had cooked up years ago.

The girls had little time to listen to the story. After the campers had all arrived, McKenzie gathered her group and Bailey went off with her group. She was learning fast under Emma's teaching. Since arriving at Sunshine Stables, she had her horse making tighter turns around the barrels, and she had also improved on her time.

After Kids' Camp, McKenzie worked diligently with Sahara. They ran through the course several times as she worked on perfecting her turns. After turning around the third and last barrel, she squeezed her calves together, urging her horse faster and faster. Emma said she was improving every day, but McKenzie wasn't sure. She hoped she placed higher in the standings than she had the previous year.

McKenzie practiced until a pickup pulled into the driveway next to the arena. She rode over to the fence, watching Maggie Preston climb out and stride toward Emma.

"Looks like you're keeping busy training your girls," Maggie said as she flipped her hair over her shoulder. "Honestly, Emma, I don't know how you can concentrate with all the commotion going on around here. I would be a basket case if my prize horse was stolen."

"I figure I have to keep busy. I just can't sit and worry, or I'd go nuts," Emma explained. "I have faith that God will return Diamond Girl to me. If I didn't have faith, I could never get through this."

Maggie shook her head and scoffed. "You need a little more than faith, Emma. It sounds to me like you need a little luck on your side. Has the sheriff found anything, yet?"

"He's working on it, but so far there's not much to go on," Emma said dismally, ignoring Maggie's comment.

"It's such a shame. Unless the sheriff finds your horse soon, you'll have to drop out of the competition, and I would sure hate to see that happen. Let's see, you've brought home the first-place trophy for three years now, right?" Maggie said as she stared intently at Emma.

"Just barely," Emma said with a smile. "You were only a fraction of a second behind me, remember?"

"How could I forget?" Maggie mumbled as she pulled her ringing cell phone from its case.

Seconds later Maggie excused herself and headed

back to her pickup. She was needed back at the stables, she said.

Emma turned to the girls and said they had worked enough for one day, so they watered the horses and turned them into the corral.

By the time they finished, a few clouds had rolled in, bringing a cool breeze with them. McKenzie suggested that she and Bailey walk to the spot in the back pasture where they had found the horseshoe earlier.

"Hopefully that yellow thing we saw in the picture is still there," McKenzie said after stopping at the house for a couple of popsicles.

"We definitely need a clue to solve this mystery, that's for sure." Bailey licked a grape popsicle. Her lips and tongue turned purple. "We don't have much to go on, yet."

"Just the horseshoe," McKenzie said, "and the yellow thingy on the ground."

"Don't forget the funny guy we saw yesterday on that gorgeous horse. That could be a clue. Maybe."

"I guess there are a few more possible clues than I thought. It would help if we could figure out if any of them are connected." McKenzie dropped a piece of strawberry popsicle on her white T-shirt. When she tried to wipe it off, the red stain grew bigger.

The fence by the creek was over a mile away and

by the time the girls reached it, sweat was dripping down McKenzie's neck. She cupped the cool water and splashed her face and arms. While Bailey dipped her arms in the creek, McKenzie walked to the fence. Hopefully, the yellow object they had seen in the photo hadn't blown away.

McKenzie stared at the ground as she walked but soon stopped and turned to her friend. "Bailey, the yellow thing is still here."

Scurrying the last few steps, McKenzie knelt and grabbed the piece of yellow plastic. She turned it over in her hand as Bailey came up behind her.

"What is it?" Bailey asked.

McKenzie looked up at Bailey, whose bangs were plastered to her head with sweat. "It's a clip used to fix a barbed-wire fence."

McKenzie stood and examined the fence beside her. Farmers and ranchers used these kinds of clips all the time. She looked up and down the fence row and saw clips on every post, securing the wire to the post. All of the other clips though had faded from the sun, but the one she held in her hand was shiny and new. She looked at the post directly in front of her. All of the clips on that post looked brand-new, too.

"I think I know how Diamond Girl got out. Someone

has recently fixed this fence. I can tell because this post has all new clips," McKenzie explained to Bailey. "The horse thief or thieves took down this stretch of fence that crosses the shallow part of the creek. After they took Diamond Girl through the opening, they fixed the fence."

Bailey's eyes lit up. "That's why there are no tracks. The thief led Diamond Girl up the creek."

McKenzie nodded. "Right. The thief struggled with Diamond Girl on the rocks in the creek. That made her lose her horseshoe back there."

"I think our detective work is paying off," Bailey said excitedly. "It's a good thing you took those pictures. Otherwise we never would have seen that clip on the ground."

McKenzie's heart beat faster as a sudden thought came to her. Someone had fixed Emma's fence, but who? Was it one of her workers? If so, did that mean someone at Sunshine Stables had stolen Diamond Girl?

McKenzie swallowed as she thought about it. All of Emma's employees were also her friends and surely none of them would steal Diamond Girl—would they?

Danger Nearby!

"Do you really think someone at Sunshine Stables stole Diamond Girl?" Bailey asked after McKenzie explained her idea.

"I don't want to believe that," McKenzie said firmly. "Everyone there loves Emma and Diamond Girl too much. At least I hope they do."

The thought that the thief might be someone McKenzie knew made her sick to her stomach. She had known most of Emma's workers for several years, except for Derek. Surely none of them would steal Emma's prize horse. But she knew she couldn't overlook this possible clue if they wanted to find Diamond Girl.

"Didn't Derek say he wanted to open his own stable someday? He said he needed a lot of money. You don't think he'd—" Bailey stopped abruptly.

"No. Derek would never steal Diamond Girl," McKenzie said as convincingly as she could. But she had also only known Derek for a couple of months.

McKenzie shook her head as she brushed the thought from her mind.

"What are we going to do?" Bailey asked.

"I don't know. I know it's wrong to accuse someone of a crime when we can't prove it, but this sure looks suspicious. I think we need to tell Emma about it." McKenzie headed up the bank toward home.

"Too bad Elizabeth's not here," Bailey said. "She would know what to do."

Besides being the oldest, Elizabeth knew her Bible much better than McKenzie did. When McKenzie read her Bible, she often didn't understand what God was saying. Elizabeth, however, always seemed to know what the scripture meant.

McKenzie sighed. "Maybe we should e-mail Elizabeth when we get back. We can tell Emma what we've found later."

McKenzie gazed across the pasture to Sunshine Stables in the distance. She wished they had ridden horses. Not only were her legs tired, but the breeze from earlier had died. A timber ran along one edge of the pasture, stretching all the way to the stables. Though walking through the trees was a longer route home, at least it was shade. So, she made a quick decision.

McKenzie looked at Bailey's red sweaty face and said,

"Let's go to the woods and cool off a little. Then we'll walk home through the trees."

Bailey eagerly agreed and in a few minutes the girls stepped into the cool shade of the timber, slumping onto a fallen log.

McKenzie laid back on the rough bark and closed her eyes. She breathed the fresh smell of grass and wildflowers and listened to the rustle of the leaves overhead. She heard the crackling sounds of rabbits and squirrels scurrying over dried twigs and grass.

The air in the timber was so still she started to doze. Then she was startled by a loud voice and the heavy clomping footsteps crunching through the brush.

McKenzie sat up and peered through the overgrown brush. Across the fence, she saw a horse and rider going through the timber. As the pair drew nearer, the horse whinnied softly.

McKenzie recognized the rider as the young man she and Bailey had seen the day before. At least McKenzie thought it was the same man. Today he wore a black cowboy hat pulled down low over his forehead, and though the day was hot, he wore a dark brown, long-sleeved shirt. His collar was pulled up to his chin, so it was hard to see his face. He was definitely riding the same horse, but he seemed to have more control of her.

Bailey whispered into McKenzie's ear, "Why is he riding out here?"

McKenzie turned to her friend. "I don't know. This is a weird place to learn to ride. I wonder if Maggie knows he's out here. I'd think she'd want her new riders to stay on open land, not in timber."

McKenzie wanted to call out to the man, but then she remembered how he had treated them. She was afraid he'd get angry again, so she decided to keep quiet. Slipping to the ground as quietly as she could, she motioned for Bailey to do the same. From behind bushes, the girls peered at the man on the spotted horse.

Again McKenzie thought there was something familiar about that horse. Why couldn't she figure out where she had seen it before?

The crunching twigs and dried leaves beneath the horse's hooves echoed through the timber. Slowly the man guided the horse around stumps and fallen logs, staring at the ground, first one side and then the other.

He acted as if he'd dropped something and was looking for it. He continued searching the ground but finally gave up. With a flick of the reins, he disappeared through the trees.

McKenzie stood and brushed the dirt from the knees of her jeans. "I wonder who that guy is." She picked a bramble off her shirt. "I think it's the same guy we saw before, but I'm not sure."

Bailey nodded. "But it's definitely the same horse."

"That horse is one of a kind, that's for sure," McKenzie said as she glanced at her watch. Chore time had probably already started, but if they hurried they would get there in time to help with most of the jobs. The girls started back toward Sunshine Stables, hurrying through the trees, dodging bushes, and low-hanging branches.

As they hurried single file through the woods, Bailey lagged behind. "Hey, McKenzie, wait up," she called through jagged breaths. "I found something." McKenzie turned and went to Bailey's side. The younger girl took a deep breath and handed McKenzie a piece of paper.

McKenzie looked at the words scrawled across it, "Willow Ridge Horse Therapy Ranch. 555-9814."

"I wonder if this was what that guy lost," McKenzie said as she studied the handwriting.

McKenzie had never heard of Willow Ridge Horse Therapy Ranch. In fact, she didn't know of a horse therapy farm around here. She stuffed the paper in her jeans and continued through the timber. Soon they arrived at Sunshine Stables. The stable hands had just begun chores, so the girls weren't late after all.

They rinsed their horses in the wash area, and

McKenzie let the cold water splash her arms and face. Usually washing the horses wasn't her favorite part of grooming, but today she enjoyed the job. The cool spray of water felt good on her sweaty skin. She didn't care that she was nearly soaked when they finished.

When the chores were finally done, the girls changed into dry shorts and T-shirts and settled in the porch swing. McKenzie pushed her toes against the wooden floor, setting the swing in motion. The heavy chain hanging from the ceiling creaked with each sway. Cicadas sang their shrill song in the nearby trees.

McKenzie leaned her head back remembering the stories the young campers had told that morning. Several of them knew people who had seen the ghost rider recently.

"I wonder if the ghost rider really has returned." McKenzie tucked one leg beneath her.

"Lots of people seem to think so." Bailey slapped a mosquito on her leg.

"I think it's funny that no one has seen this ghost rider for years. Now, all of a sudden he shows up again, right after Diamond Girl disappears. Don't you think it's weird?" McKenzie looked skeptically at Bailey.

Bailey nodded. "Yeah, I guess it is. It's all a part of the mystery."

McKenzie thought about Bailey's words. Maybe the ghost rider was a part of Diamond Girl's disappearance. It seemed more than coincidence that the mysterious rider had shown up this week. Did he know something about the horse? McKenzie was still wondering about that when Emma called them in for supper.

While they ate, McKenzie told Emma what the campers had told them that morning. "Do you think the ghost rider could be back?"

Emma laid down her hamburger before speaking. "Oh, I'm sure those people really did see someone. There are several riding stables around here, you know. Old Towne belongs to Sunshine Stables, but some people forget it's private property. I wouldn't be surprised if someone was riding out there, but I think it's just the old story coming back to life. I suppose I need to put up some new 'No Trespassing' signs, though."

The three continued eating in silence.

"Have you heard anything new from the sheriff about Diamond Girl?" Bailey interrupted the silence as she set down her milk glass.

Emma shook her head. "Instead of branding my horses, I have microchips embedded in their necks. Now, if the thief tries to sell Diamond Girl at a horse auction, the microchip will be scanned, and it will show that she has been stolen. Authorities can then be called to make an arrest. The sheriff is hoping the thief will eventually show up at one of these auctions. He doesn't really have any other leads on the case."

Bailey stuffed her last bite of hamburger into her mouth. "I sure hope we find her soon."

Emma nodded as she stared at her plate. "The longer it takes to find Diamond Girl, the farther the thief can take her."

"Keep praying about it, Emma," Bailey encouraged. "Doesn't God answer all our prayers if we have faith?"

McKenzie hadn't noticed the dark circles beneath Emma's eyes until now. McKenzie knew how much her instructor loved her horse, and she could tell Emma hadn't been sleeping much. McKenzie felt a lump form in the bottom of her stomach.

"You're right, Bailey," Emma said after a moment. "God does answer all prayers, but He doesn't always give us what we ask for. He gives us what He knows is best for us."

McKenzie stacked the empty plates and carried them to the sink. She knew Emma's words were true. But she felt God was directing her to keep searching for Diamond Girl.

"Emma, would you care if Bailey and I go out to Old Towne before it gets dark?" McKenzie rinsed the dishes and placed them in the dishwasher.

"Sure, go ahead," Emma said with a slight smile. "But you girls have done enough walking for one day. Since the horses are put away for the night, why don't you take the four-wheelers? You have driven one haven't you, Bailey?"

"I drove one several times at the stable where I practice back home," Bailey said.

"Good." Emma turned to McKenzie. "You can show Bailey the smaller four-wheelers. Be careful and don't be gone long."

Minutes later McKenzie led the way to the machine shed and stepped inside. She grabbed two helmets, giving one to Bailey.

McKenzie pointed to a small four-wheeler. "That one's for you," she said. She hopped on the seat of a red ATV that she had ridden many times before.

Bailey climbed onto the blue four-wheeler. As the girls pressed the starter buttons, the engines roared to life. McKenzie steered her ATV through the large doorway and motioned for Bailey to follow. Soon, both girls were headed down the tree-lined path that led to Old Towne.

The sun hung low in the sky, casting long dark shadows. Mosquitoes buzzed around their heads while vultures hovered on the ground ahead of them. They flapped their heavy wings and soared into the sky when they heard the roar of the engines.

At the top of the hill overlooking Old Towne, McKenzie steered her ATV into a small thicket of trees and parked.

"Why did you want to come out here?" Bailey asked as she turned off her four-wheeler.

"I thought maybe we could watch for the ghost rider or find signs that someone has been here." McKenzie set her helmet on the seat of the four-wheeler and headed down the slope. "Our four-wheelers are pretty much hidden here in the trees. Let's go on down and look around. We don't have much time before dusk, and that's when everyone has seen the ghost rider."

"Where are we going to hide so we can watch for him?" Bailey jogged to catch up with McKenzie.

"See that slope just past the old schoolhouse? I thought we could crouch low on the other side. Nobody could see us there." McKenzie pointed to an area about 100 yards away.

Soon the girls were walking down the only street in Old Towne. The Old West setup reminded McKenzie of ghost towns she had seen in movies. The town was eerily quiet in the gloom. The entire street was shrouded in shadows. Old shutters banged on upstairs windows, and the old windmill creaked as the wind turned its blades. McKenzie felt goose bumps ripple up her arms.

"This is creepy," Bailey whispered as she edged closer to McKenzie.

"I agree," McKenzie whispered back. "Let's get to our lookout."

Eager to get out of Old Towne, the girls scurried down the street past the schoolhouse. McKenzie reached the top of the slope first and stopped. The ground before them had suddenly dropped off. She instinctively flung out her arm to keep Bailey from falling over the edge.

McKenzie peered over the edge. Something was strange about this place. She knew there were no cliffs out here, so what caused this drop-off? Then an idea came to her as she scurried down the side of the hill. Soon she was standing below Bailey looking up at her friend.

"Bailey, come down here," McKenzie called. "You've got to see this. It's an old pioneer dugout. You're standing on the roof."

Bailey giggled and scurried to McKenzie's side. "Wow. Is this ever cool."

"I don't think it was used as a house, though," McKenzie said. "Look at the wide double doors. I think it was a stable."

McKenzie stepped to the old rickety door and

pulled on it. It creaked on rusty hinges as McKenzie peered inside. It took her eyes a moment to adjust to the darkness and then she exclaimed, "Look Bailey. There's fresh hay in here."

"Do you think someone is keeping a horse here?" Bailey whispered.

McKenzie eyed an old wooden feed bunk. Bits of leftover feed lay in it, and a large bucket of clean water stood in the corner. McKenzie's heart fluttered as she glanced about the dark, musty stable.

"It sure looks like it," McKenzie said. She poked around in another bucket and found a lead rope, curry comb, and other grooming supplies. A larger third bucket held empty diet pop cans, candy, and fast food wrappers, an empty bottle of hair dye, and dirty stained rags.

McKenzie jumped as a gust of wind blew the stable door shut. Her heart thumped loudly in her chest as she put a finger to her lips. "Did you hear that?" she whispered.

"I just heard the banging door." Bailey clutched McKenzie's arm. "What did you hear?"

"It sounded like a horse neighing." McKenzie pushed the door open and peered out cautiously. After glancing in all directions, she stepped outside.

The sun had sunk below the horizon, deepening the

shadows and darkness. For a moment she thought she heard rustling in the nearby timber. She squinted but saw nothing besides trees and a meadow. Yet, something didn't feel right. She had the feeling something or someone was watching her.

Suddenly, waiting for the ghost rider didn't seem like such a good idea.

McKenzie reached into the dugout and clutched Bailey's arm. She suddenly sensed that danger lurked nearby.

"Let's get out of here before someone sees us!"

A Disturbing Discovery

McKenzie pulled Bailey away from the stable and headed up the hill. When she reached the top, she turned and looked back. The woods looked dark and scary in the fading light.

"Let's run," she said, tugging Bailey after her.

McKenzie ran as fast as she could toward Old Towne, her feet barely touching on the dirt street. In the dusk, the stores lining Main Street reminded her of a tunnel. She raced past the general store and the old wooden windmill and didn't stop until she reached the thicket of trees at the top of the hill.

She bent and placed her hands on her knees, panting as she waited for Bailey to catch up.

Bailey breathed heavily as she slowly climbed the slope, holding her side when she reached the top. "I need to rest," she said as she pulled her inhaler out of her pocket and took several deep breaths.

"I'm sorry, Bailey, but as soon as you can drive we

need to get out of here," McKenzie said nervously.

"What's the hurry?" Bailey asked as her breathing slowed.

"I'll tell you when we get home. Let's go." McKenzie hopped on her four-wheeler and steered it onto the dirt track. McKenzie looked behind to make sure Bailey was following; then she sped up the path.

Lightning bugs flickered in the twilight while the beams from her headlight cast eerie shadows along the path. A chilly wind had replaced the heat from earlier in the day, making McKenzie wish she had worn a sweatshirt. Within a few minutes she saw the lights of Sunshine Stables.

Driving into the machine shed, she flipped on the overhead light. When both girls had parked their ATVs, they settled onto some old wooden crates. McKenzie rubbed her arms to chase away the chill.

"Okay, tell me now." Bailey pulled her knees to her chest and stretched her T-shirt over her legs. "Did you see something? Did you see the ghost rider?"

"Well, I know I heard a horse. It sounded like it was coming from the timber by the dugout. I know we went out there to try to see the ghost rider, but then I decided it might not be a good idea," McKenzie explained.

"But why?" Bailey looked quizzically at McKenzie.

"That was the whole point of going to Old Towne."

"I know, but if we see the ghost rider and he knows we saw him, he won't come back. Right? I think there's a connection between the ghost rider and Diamond Girl's disappearance. We need to find out more about him and why he's hanging around Old Towne. If we scare him off, we'll never solve this mystery."

"I guess you're right," Bailey said as she stepped off the crate. She picked up Cheetah who had wandered into the shed. The cat settled into her arms and closed her eyes. "So, what now?"

"I don't know." McKenzie sighed and then added, "Maybe that note you found earlier has another clue on it."

"Yeah," Bailey said as she stroked Cheetah's back. "You put it in your pocket."

"I sure hope Emma didn't do laundry this evening." McKenzie hopped off the crate and headed for the door. "I'd better go find it."

Within minutes the girls were in the house and racing up the stairs to their bedroom, McKenzie taking them two at a time.

"Oh, good. They're just where I left them." She grabbed her jeans off the floor and pulled the scrap of paper out of the pocket.

She unfolded the crumpled paper and turned it over.

"All it says is Willow Ridge Horse Therapy Ranch and the phone number. There's nothing written on the back, either."

She opened the dresser drawer and tucked it under her socks for safekeeping. The note must be important if the man was looking for it. But then she thought maybe it wasn't even his. Maybe he had been looking for something else.

McKenzie sighed. If the sheriff had no clues to Diamond Girl's disappearance, would Bailey and she really be able to help? She wondered if searching for clues was a waste of time. It was only a few more days until the rodeo, and then she would leave Sunshine Stables. What if she left before finding out what happened to Emma's horse? She promised herself she wouldn't let that happen.

"Do you think we should tell Emma we suspect Derek?" Bailey asked, interrupting McKenzie's thoughts.

McKenzie frowned. She still didn't want to think Derek was involved with Diamond Girl's disappearance. "We were going to ask Elizabeth about that, weren't we?" she asked

"Why don't you call her instead?" Bailey asked.

McKenzie agreed and quickly called their friend in Texas, explaining the situation to Elizabeth.

"I don't think you should mention Derek's name to anybody yet," Elizabeth said. "After all, you don't have any evidence against him, just hunches. You shouldn't wrongfully accuse him or anyone else."

McKenzie knew Elizabeth was right, so they chatted a few more minutes. She was just hanging up as Emma called up the stairs. She had popped popcorn and invited them to watch a movie with her before bed. The girls readily agreed and scampered downstairs.

During the first commercial break, McKenzie planned to ask Emma about the dugout at Old Towne, but when she glanced over at her instructor in the recliner, she noticed Emma's eyes were closed. Her breathing was soft and regular. McKenzie knew Emma was exhausted, so she dimmed the lights and turned off the TV. She put her finger to her lips and motioned for Bailey to follow her upstairs.

When the girls woke the next morning, Emma had already gone to the stables to prepare for the last day of Kids' Camp. After a quick breakfast, McKenzie and Bailey headed outside to help feed Sahara and the other horses that weren't used for camp. When the young campers arrived, they fed and groomed the horses they used for camp.

At two o'clock the campers went home. Emma had

told McKenzie and Bailey they could ride the four-wheelers across the meadow to Cedar Creek Ranch to watch the roping class. The girls arrived early, hoping to walk through the stables and see Maggie's horses. They were eager to see if the beautiful spotted horse was in one of her stalls.

After parking their four-wheelers, the girls spotted Maggie outside the stables.

"Hi, Maggie," McKenzie called out as they approached Cedar Creek's owner.

"Hi, girls. You're early. The riders won't be here for another twenty minutes," she said, glancing at her watch.

"We know," McKenzie replied. "We were wondering if we could look at your horses."

Maggie hesitated but then said, "I suppose that would be okay, but I don't have time to take you on a tour. I have to get the calves into the corral for the couple coming to practice. You can go by yourselves if you keep out of the way of my workers."

The girls promised they wouldn't bother anyone and set off toward the stable. McKenzie led the way inside and headed down the first aisle, glancing in the stalls as she walked. They passed quarter horses and paint horses with beautiful white splotches on their coats. They saw spotted Appaloosas and sturdy Morgans. She recognized

Maggie's black mustang in a stall at the end.

"This is Maggie's prize horse, Frisco." McKenzie stepped aside so Bailey could see in the stall. "She's almost as fast as Diamond Girl."

"Yeah," Bailey said. "Maggie made it clear yesterday that Emma always beats her."

McKenzie nodded. "But, second place is really good, too."

"You don't know what it's like to always come in second, or worse. I never win anything." Bailey frowned.

At first, McKenzie didn't know what to say. She knew how Bailey felt. "Bailey," McKenzie finally said softly, "you'll win lots of things. It's just that I've been riding a lot longer than you have, and I'm older. I did awful at last year's rodeo, so I do know how you feel. But you have lots of talents and abilities. I've seen some of your drawings and they're great. I can't draw a good stick man."

Bailey sighed but didn't answer. The girls continued down the aisle as McKenzie pointed out several breeds of horses to Bailey. She hoped to see the beautiful spotted horse they had seen in the pasture, but it wasn't in the first row of stalls. When they walked up the second aisle, they saw no sign of her there either.

Disappointed that they hadn't seen the unusual horse, McKenzie began to wonder who owned it. And why was the rider on Maggie's land if the horse wasn't stabled there? McKenzie was puzzled as she glanced at her watch and moved quickly through the stable.

The girls arrived back at the arena as Maggie turned the calves into the ring. McKenzie climbed the fence and sat on the top rung, while Bailey stood beside her.

A pair of girls, a little older than McKenzie, sat on a brown stallion. They chased a calf around the arena, the rider in front holding a lasso. As they approached a calf she flung the lasso, catching it around the calf's neck. Then she jerked the rope flinging the calf to the ground.

Bailey jumped and cried out, "Doesn't that hurt the calf?"

"Nope, not at all," McKenzie assured her as they watched the girls slip to the ground and loop the other end of rope around the calf's legs. "Just wait a sec and you'll see."

Moments later, after the calf laid still, Maggie stepped out and loosened the rope. After Maggie removed the lasso, the calf hopped up and ran around the arena unharmed.

"Maybe I could do that," Bailey said with a grin. "Now that I know it doesn't hurt the calf."

"Great," McKenzie said. "Maybe I can find an old rope around here, and I can practice throwing a lasso."

McKenzie glanced behind her, looking for Maggie. She heard voices coming from an old garage, so she tugged on Bailey's arm and headed in that direction. As they stepped inside she saw stacks of cardboard boxes, with the contents written with black marker on the outside. Two workers carried the boxes out the back door and loaded them into a trailer parked nearby. They paid no attention to the girls but continued hauling the boxes out.

McKenzie turned to Bailey and whispered, "I wonder what's going on in here."

Bailey pointed to the men cleaning out the garage. "Where do you think they're taking all that stuff?"

"I don't know, but it looks almost like they're getting ready to move." McKenzie eyed all the busyness around her. "Surely, Maggie's not moving. Emma hasn't said anything about it."

"I bet they're just cleaning out the garage," Bailey said as she stepped away from the garage.

"Could be," McKenzie said skeptically. "They look too busy to help us find a rope. We should probably head back anyway, but I need to find Maggie and thank her for letting us come over."

McKenzie glanced around the arena looking for Maggie. She was nowhere in sight, so the girls headed toward the stables to look for her. Stable hands were doing nightly chores. McKenzie pulled Bailey into the supply room to let two workers pass with wheelbarrows full of hay.

McKenzie turned and noticed the shelves were nearly bare and cardboard boxes lined the floor. All of them were filled with horse supplies.

She jumped at a harsh voice behind them. "What do you need, girls?"

McKenzie turned to see Maggie standing in the doorway. The woman drained the last of her diet cola can and tossed it into the trashcan.

"Uh, we just wanted to thank you for letting us come over," McKenzie stammered.

"Yeah, it was really nice of you," Bailey agreed. "I think I can do the calf-roping thing after watching those girls. Will you be at the rodeo to watch us?"

Maggie shooed the girls out of the room. She smirked at Bailey and replied, "Oh, I think I'll be there, all right."

"Are you moving, Maggie?" McKenzie asked as she glanced at the boxes.

Maggie hesitated and peered around as though to see if anyone was standing nearby. Then she pulled the girls closer and said in a near whisper, "I have someone coming over to look at the place and want it to look nice, so I'm cleaning out some junk. Nothing is definite yet; so don't say anything about it. Not even to Emma. Okay?"

The girls looked at each other, but agreed not to say anything. McKenzie wondered why in the world Maggie wanted to keep it a secret, especially from Emma. She thought the two women were friends. Another thought crept into McKenzie's mind. *Maggie acts like she's got something to hide. Would she have stolen Diamond Girl to keep Emma from winning the rodeo?*

Then Maggie motioned for the girls to step outside and continued, "I'm glad I could help you girls, but you better go home." Before the girls could respond, the woman turned and started to walk away.

"Oh, I almost forgot," Maggie said. She turned back to the girls and pulled a folded newspaper page from her back pocket. "Would you give this paper to Derek? I circled an ad I thought he might want to see."

McKenzie assured Maggie she would give the paper to Derek, and minutes later the girls headed for home. After parking the ATVs, McKenzie unfolded the newspaper and glanced at the ad Maggie had circled in bright red ink.

"Look at this, Bailey." McKenzie pointed to the ad. "Maggie wanted Derek to see this ad about a stable for sale in northern Montana."

Bailey skimmed the ad. "I thought he wasn't going to buy a stable until he'd saved more money."

"I thought so, too," McKenzie agreed.

Bailey was silent for a moment. Then she spoke softly. "Maybe he sold something worth a lot of money."

McKenzie looked up. "You don't think Derek stole Diamond Girl and sold her, do you?"

"I know you like him, McKenzie," Bailey said. "But he has a reason to steal her. He wants money to buy a stable. Remember the other day when he said certain thieves knew how to disguise a horse. He knows how to do all those tricks with horses. Maybe he's disguised Diamond Girl."

McKenzie knew Bailey was right about one thing. She did like Derek. He had always been so nice, helping her feed and groom Sahara. He always seemed happy to have her around the stables.

Though she hated to admit it, he did have a reason to steal Diamond Girl. But that didn't mean he was the thief, did it? More than anything she wanted to prove Derek was innocent, but she didn't know how. All the clues seemed to point toward his guilt.

She felt torn inside. What if she accused Derek and he was innocent? Could she forgive herself? But more importantly, would God forgive her?

The Nighttime Adventure

The weekend passed with no news or leads to Diamond Girl's disappearance. McKenzie began to wonder if she would ever learn what had happened to the prize horse. She knew God wanted her to help solve the mystery, but she also knew He expected her to not wrongly accuse anyone. Part of her was scared to meet the thief face-to-face. What if he was someone she knew and trusted? Would she be able to continue loving that person as God would want her to?

After church on Sunday, McKenzie pushed the thoughts from her mind as she headed to the arena to practice for the rodeo. She watched Bailey as she raced the barrel course with Applejack. Bailey had improved much since coming to Sunshine Stables, and McKenzie hoped she would do well at the rodeo. Placing in the top three would mean a lot to Bailey.

Soon it was McKenzie's turn to race with Sahara. As she leaned forward, the warm evening air caught her ponytail, slapping it up and down. Again and again she raced. Each time she worked on tightening her turns. Then she took a break and it was Bailey's turn again.

Finally Emma said the girls had practiced enough for one night. McKenzie sighed with relief. It had been a long day and she was ready to go inside. She hadn't chatted online with the Camp Club girls for a couple of days, so she wanted to fill them in on all the happenings.

Minutes later McKenzie and Bailey sat in front of Emma's computer. The other four Camp Club girls were already chatting online.

McKenzie: *LTNC.*

Elizabeth: *Where have U 2 been?*

McKenzie: *Busy with horses and trying to figure out what happened to Diamond Girl.*

Alexis: *Do you have any clues?*

McKenzie: *We found a fence clip near the place in the creek where we found the horseshoe. Someone cut the fence and fixed it with clips. The thief could've stolen DG from that spot and led her up creek.*

I don't want 2 suspect Derek, but he has a reason to steal DG. He needs $$ 2 buy his own stable.

Bailey took over the keyboard: *And twice we've seen a stranger riding that beautiful spotted horse. I've never seen one like it. He acts funny 2. Doesn't even know the horse's name and he couldn't even control her.*

Kate: *U know U can lead a horse 2 water but U can't make him drink.*

Elizabeth: *Reminds me of my mom's favorite song, "Horse with No Name."*

Sydney: *UR horse with no name is a horse of a different color, LOL.*

McKenzie thought about her friends' remarks. From the first time she saw the strange horse, she thought it looked familiar. Now she knew why.

McKenzie: *U guys made me realize something. If that horse was black and didn't have spots, she could B DG!*

Kate: *Could someone have dyed DG's coat?*

McKenzie and Bailey looked at each other. Both wondered if it could be possible. McKenzie remembered the bottle of hair dye in the dugout.

McKenzie: *Dunno. How could we tell?*

Kate: *If u can get some hairs from horse I could test it with my kit.*

McKenzie knew Kate loved anything technical. She saved all her birthday and Christmas money to buy the latest gadgets. Kate was a whiz with computers and electronics. McKenzie knew Kate could test the horse hair, but she wondered how she could get the hair in the first place.

"Girls, it's getting late," a voice behind them called.

McKenzie glanced behind her. Emma was leaning against the door frame, smiling at them.

"Okay, we'll sign off," McKenzie said.

McKenzie: *G2G. Thx GFs. TTFN.*

After the girls logged off, they headed upstairs.

"Do you think the spotted horse could actually be Diamond Girl?" Bailey asked as she slipped into her pajamas.

McKenzie climbed onto the top bunk. "I suppose it's possible. Everybody assumes the thief would take Diamond Girl far away. But, what better way to hide her than in plain sight."

Bailey crawled beneath the covers. "Do you think the thief is hiding the spotted horse in the dugout stable at Old Towne?"

"I've wondered about that. It sure looked like someone was keeping a horse there." McKenzie flipped onto her stomach and peered over the edge of the bed. "If so, I bet it's bedded down there at night."

Bailey peered up at McKenzie with questioning eyes. "What are you getting at?"

McKenzie flung her hair out of her eyes and grinned. "I think we need to see if a horse is out there!"

Bailey's eyes grew wide. "You mean now?"

"If that horse is actually Diamond Girl, the thief won't keep her there forever. We need to find out before she disappears again." McKenzie felt her pulse quicken. She wasn't sure she wanted to go to Old Towne after dark, but she knew they had to. In just a few short days, they would leave Sunshine Stables to go back to their homes. If they wanted to solve the mystery of Diamond Girl's disappearance, they had to hurry. "Hopefully, the spotted horse is there, and we can snip some hairs to send to Kate."

Bailey stared at McKenzie. "Well, if you're going, I'm not going to wait here," she said.

It was just after ten o'clock. If they took the horses, they could go to Old Towne, check the place out, and easily be back in less than an hour. She jumped from the top bunk. In a couple of minutes both girls had changed into jeans and sweatshirts.

The house was dark when they stepped into the hallway. They paused outside Emma's bedroom door, but no sounds came from within. McKenzie knew they should ask for permission, but she hated to wake Emma.

McKenzie made a quick decision. She motioned for Bailey to follow her as she tiptoed down the stairs. The yard light cast a soft glow through the windows, so they could make their way through the house.

McKenzie flipped on the light over the kitchen sink

and pulled a pair of small scissors, a zippered sandwich bag, and a pocket flashlight out of a drawer. She shoved them into her sweatshirt pocket as she stepped into the mud room. After grabbing a battery-powered lantern, the girls quietly slipped outside.

McKenzie shivered in the cool breeze. She was glad she had worn her sweatshirt. The yard light cast eerie shadows in the corners of the yard. Leaves in the treetops rustled in the wind, and the bushes scratched against the house.

The girls ran to the stable and slipped inside as McKenzie flipped on the light switch. She heard the steady breathing of the horses, their bodies thumping against the dividers as they settled in their stalls. McKenzie wished she could sit down right here to spend the night, but she knew she had to finish what they intended to do. After grabbing Sahara's saddle from the tack room, McKenzie lugged it into the stall.

Sahara blinked sleepily at McKenzie as she stepped inside. McKenzie talked to the horse as she set the saddle on her back. "It's okay, girl. We're going to go for a ride." McKenzie reached beneath the mare and secured the saddle. She patted the horse's head and led her out of the stall.

"Let's both ride Sahara," McKenzie suggested. "It'll be quicker. Then you can hold the lantern. Okay?"

Relief flooded Bailey's face. "Good. I didn't really want to ride after dark by myself."

McKenzie continued down the hallway and out the stable door with Sahara. She put her foot in the stirrup and mounted the horse. Then she pulled Bailey into the saddle behind her. They headed out of the lot and onto the trail.

After they passed behind the pine grove away from the yard light, she could see the sprinkling of stars in the black sky. The half-sized moon cast enough light so they could find their way without using the lantern. Twisted shadows from a maze of trees fell across the ground. McKenzie shivered beneath her sweatshirt. She felt Bailey wrap her small arms around her waist.

"Are you sure we should do this?" Bailey asked softly. "It's creepy out here."

McKenzie agreed with Bailey. This was the spookiest thing she had ever done. But with all the confidence she could gather, she said, "We have to do this, for Diamond Girl and for Emma."

"Okay, but let's get this over with as fast as we can," Bailey said. "I don't like it out here."

McKenzie turned her head toward Bailey. "We're almost there," she whispered as she saw the buildings of Old Towne.

Main Street, with its tall empty stores on either side, surrounded them in a blanket of darkness. Sahara plodded down the street, her thumping hooves the only sound in the gloom. As they rounded the curve outside of the town, McKenzie headed up the slope overlooking the dugout. She slid to the ground and looped Sahara's reins around a tree branch.

McKenzie felt as if they were in the middle of nowhere with meadow in all directions. The mountains on the horizon made her feel even more isolated. Coyotes yipped in the distance and an owl hooted. Bailey clutched McKenzie's arm.

"Let's see if the horse is in the dugout," McKenzie whispered as she led Bailey down the slope.

McKenzie put her ear to the open window of the dugout, straining to hear if something was inside. The heavy breathing of a large animal as it shifted positions came from the far corner of the dugout. Peering through the window, McKenzie flicked on her pocket light.

"It's the spotted horse," she whispered as she flicked off her light. "Someone *is* hiding her here. Let's go around front and go in."

"Oooh, McKenzie. I don't like this," Bailey said with fear in her voice.

McKenzie glanced in both directions as she pulled

Bailey to the dugout door. The rusty hinges squeaked loudly as McKenzie opened it and slipped inside.

The spotted horse stood in the corner of the dirt room. She blinked as McKenzie turned on the lantern light.

"She's even prettier up close," Bailey said with awe.

McKenzie walked cautiously to the horse's side and held out her hand, talking to her in a soothing voice. The horse nuzzled McKenzie's hand.

"Oh, Bailey. Her eyes look just like Diamond Girl's. She acts like her, too."

McKenzie stroked the large white spot on the horse's forehead. She examined it closely. Had someone dyed the hair brown and turned the diamond shape into an uneven splotch? Were the other spots dyed onto the horse? If so, the person had done a good job. In the dim light, the splotches of color looked natural.

She flung her arms around the horse's neck, feeling as though God had led her here for a reason. Squeezing her eyes shut, she murmured, "Dear God, let this be Diamond Girl. Please."

For a minute, McKenzie forgot her real purpose for coming here, then she pulled away from the horse as uneasiness settled over her. Though the girls were alone in the dugout, she felt as if they shouldn't be here. "Let's get this done and get back home," she said. "Do you want to hold the light or snip the hairs?"

"I'll hold the light," Bailey answered.

McKenzie dug into her pocket and pulled out the scissors. Her hands trembled as she lifted the mane and snipped some strands on the underside. After rolling the length of hair around her hand, she tucked it into the plastic bag.

McKenzie's heart leaped as a scratching sound came from outside the stable door. She stuffed the bag into her pocket and spun around. Goosebumps rippled up her arms and the scratching grew louder. Someone or something was trying to get in.

Bailey screamed and flung one hand over her mouth. She held up the light and pointed to the bottom of the stable door. A growling animal with hairy paws was digging under the door!

"What is it?" Bailey's voice trembled. She grabbed McKenzie's arm.

Before McKenzie could answer, the animal stuck its paw farther under the door. Her heart raced as she scurried to the window and cautiously stuck her head out. She pointed her pocket light at the door and gasped. Then she let out a big sigh as she yanked open the door. A bundle of fur jumped on her.

"Buckeye! You goofy dog," she said with a laugh. "Why did you follow us? You scared us half to death!"

The dog danced about their feet, yipping. He ran circles around her ankles, excited to see the girls. Bailey dropped McKenzie's arm and shook her head as she stroked Buckeye's head.

McKenzie scratched the dog's back and turned to Bailey. "We need to get going. I don't want whoever's hiding this horse here to come back and catch us."

McKenzie gave the horse a quick pat before Bailey turned off the lantern light. Buckeye scampered around their feet as they stepped outside and made their way in the moonlight to Sahara.

She couldn't wait to get away from here, back to the warmth of Emma's house. Taking a deep breath to help her relax, McKenzie mounted her horse. Then she pulled Bailey on behind her.

"I hope we don't get caught," Bailey whispered dismally. "I'm scared."

"Me, too." McKenzie turned Sahara around and headed back through Old Towne. "This place gets creepier all the time."

Buckeye ran beside the horse as the girls galloped down the dark, dusty street. Somehow, McKenzie felt safer with the dog beside them. They raced up the trail as fast as they dared in the shadowy darkness.

The dirt track seemed to go on forever, but McKenzie leaned forward, urging Sahara faster. The pounding of the horse's hooves thundered in the windy night. McKenzie sighed with relief when they crested the top of the hill and saw the yard lights of Sunshine Stables.

Emma's house was still dark. Feeling guilty for sneaking out, McKenzie moved as quickly as she could, returning Sahara to her stall. After settling her in again for the night, they scurried toward the door. McKenzie switched off the light, engulfing the stable in darkness.

As the girls stepped outside, McKenzie latched the door. She turned to follow Bailey when a movement next to the stables caught her eye. Something was there! Whirling around, she stifled a scream. A tall, dark figure stepped out of the shadows and grabbed her arm.

The Mysterious Message

McKenzie's heart raced. She heard Bailey muffle a shriek.

"Don't tell me you two can't stay away from your horses all night. You scared me silly."

McKenzie stared at the face looking down at her in the darkness, her voice quivering. "Derek, you scared *us* half to death. What are you doing out here? I thought you went home hours ago."

"I told Emma I'd patrol the ranch tonight. I just got back from making the rounds. I was heading back to my cot in the supply room, and I saw the lights in the stable go out. I thought for sure the horse thieves were back. Lucky for you I decided to check things out before calling the sheriff. Now you two better get back to bed before Emma finds out you're gone." Derek put his arms on the girls' shoulders and pushed them gently toward the house. "And stay in bed this time. I'm taking care of things out here, so you don't need to check on the horses. Good night."

The girls sighed with relief as they whispered their "good nights" to Derek and hurried into the house. They crept upstairs to their bedroom as silently as possible. McKenzie took the bag of horse hairs from her pocket and laid it on the dresser.

"Boy, that was close," Bailey said as she climbed into bed. "Do you think Derek knows we went to Old Towne?"

"I don't think so, or he would have told us. He was making rounds, so I don't think he saw a thing." McKenzie climbed into her bunk and flipped off the light switch with her foot.

Bailey whispered, "Do you think that horse was Diamond Girl?"

"I don't know, but I hope so," McKenzie said as she pulled the covers to her chin. "We need to get to town tomorrow and send those hairs to Kate by overnight mail. If it's stolen, the thief won't keep the horse there forever, so we have to move fast before he decides to move her."

"Why is that guy hiding the horse there?" Bailey asked. "If he wants her for the money, why hasn't he sold her?"

"Maybe he doesn't want to sell her. Maybe he wants to keep her for himself. She is a prize-winning rodeo horse, you know. She brings in quite a bit of money," McKenzie answered.

"Maybe he'll enter her in the rodeo," Bailey suggested. "If the horse is really Diamond Girl, no one would recognize her. She would win for sure."

The moonlight cast a soft glow about the room. McKenzie peered over the top bunk and saw Bailey's black hair framing her pale face in the dark.

McKenzie thought for a moment. "That's possible, but Emma will be at the rodeo. Surely the thief knows that. Emma would recognize Diamond Girl even if she's been dyed brown and covered with white splotches. I think we've overlooked a clue, but I don't know what it is."

"Do you think we should tell Emma that we found a horse at Old Towne?' Bailey asked.

"Yes," McKenzie agreed. "She needs to know someone is hiding a strange horse on her land. Let's tell her first thing in the morning."

•—•—•

Sunlight was beaming through the window when McKenzie woke up. She flung the covers off and stretched her legs, listening to Bailey's soft steady breathing coming from the bottom bunk.

Her eyes opened wide when she glanced at the digital clock on the desk. "Bailey," McKenzie exclaimed. "It's after nine o'clock!"

Bailey rolled over and rubbed her eyes. "We're

supposed to be doing chores. How did we sleep this late?"

McKenzie jumped out of bed and reached for her jeans. "I can't believe Emma didn't wake us. We have a lot of work to do today."

Within minutes both girls scrambled down the stairs to the kitchen. The house was quiet, so McKenzie knew Emma had probably been up for hours. Though the girls usually woke on their own, McKenzie couldn't help wondering why Emma hadn't awakened them. The girls downed some orange juice, grabbed a couple of bagels, and hurried to the stables.

At first McKenzie didn't see any stable hands. But then she saw Derek leading a caramel-colored Thoroughbred into the stable.

"Hey, Derek," McKenzie called out as she hurried down the aisle toward him. "Have you seen Emma?"

"You girls are a couple of sleepyheads. I've been waiting for you to get up." He closed the stall door behind the horse. "Why don't you ride into White Sulfur Springs with me when I go get feed. Emma had a little accident this morning."

McKenzie caught her breath. "What happened? Is she hurt bad?"

Derek opened the stable door for them as they stepped outside. "She was trying to break that little filly to ride. It threw her off, and she landed on her arm. You know Emma, she didn't want to go to the doctor, but I was afraid she broke it. She wouldn't let me take her, so I called her mom to come over. They left for the emergency room about an hour ago."

Bailey's eyes grew wide with worry. "Will she be okay?"

"I'm sure she'll be fine." Derek smiled as he walked toward his black pickup truck. "Why don't we go find her now?"

Bailey opened the passenger door of the pickup and crawled inside. Then McKenzie remembered the bag of horse hair. "I need to mail a package. Can you wait a couple of minutes while I get it ready?"

"Sure, I'll be waiting," Derek said.

McKenzie hurried toward the house with Bailey close behind her.

"We need an envelope for the hair. Hopefully, Emma has one in the office," McKenzie said as the screen door banged behind her. She hurried down the hall and into the office. She opened the supply drawer and found a brown envelope. "Perfect," she said as she grabbed it and headed upstairs.

"I'll look up Kate's address." Bailey pulled her pink and green striped address book out of her drawer. She not only had the Camp Club girls' addresses in it but also their phone numbers and e-mail addresses. Flipping the pages, she quickly found the address.

McKenzie printed Kate's name and address on the envelope, then stuffed the bag of horse hair inside. She added a short note which read, "Please hurry. We need your help—BFF, McKenzie and Bailey."

On her way out the door, McKenzie grabbed the small backpack she sometimes carried for a purse. Overnight mail would cost a lot, and she hoped she had enough money.

The girls hurried downstairs and out the door. McKenzie had a funny feeling as she crawled in the pickup beside Derek. She felt guilty wondering if he was a horse thief. Then she remembered that her dad had once told her that guilt was God's way of speaking to His children. Was God trying to tell her something now about Derek?

As she leaned her head back in the seat, her mind wandered. They needed to solve the mystery of Diamond Girl's disappearance, but they also needed to focus on the rodeo that started tomorrow. In the afternoon, the judging of the Junior Miss Rodeo Queen contest would begin. She would be judged on her appearance, personality, and how well she handled her horse while riding. She shuddered at the thought of standing before the judges.

"You two are awfully quiet this morning," Derek said, interrupting her thoughts. "Did you have too late of a night last night?"

"We just have a lot to think about," Bailey answered.

McKenzie stared out the window at the distant mountains. About twenty minutes later Derek pulled into the parking lot of Mountainview Medical Center.

McKenzie wrinkled her nose at the smell of antiseptic as she stepped inside the hospital. Derek stopped at the front desk and asked the receptionist about Emma. After listening to her directions, the girls followed Derek down the hallway to a small room. A middle-aged blond-haired woman who looked like an older version of Emma smiled at them as they entered.

Emma sat on the bed with her arm in a sling, her eyes rimmed by dark circles. "Hey, girls, Derek." She held out her uninjured arm toward the girls.

McKenzie stepped to Emma's side and put her arms around her. Emma winced.

"I'm sorry, Emma," McKenzie said. "Did I hurt you?"

"No, no," Emma said, forcing a smile to her face. "I'm fine."

"What did the doc say?" Derek asked. "Is your arm broken?"

"Just a sprain, but I get a sling anyway." Emma shifted,

holding her arm gingerly. "I also get to spend the night here. The doctor wants to make sure I don't have a concussion."

She looked apologetically at Derek and the girls. "I'm really sorry about all this, guys. I know it's bad timing with the rodeo almost here."

"Don't worry about anything," Derek said. "We'll take care of things at the stables."

"I'm waiting for the nurse to come back and take me to my room," Emma said with a frown.

Emma's mom, Mrs. Wilson, turned to the girls. "Emma asked me to stay with you girls tonight. If that's okay with you, I'll be out to the house after she gets settled here."

The girls told Mrs. Wilson that would be fine. They said their good-byes and headed back to the pickup. McKenzie asked Derek if he would drop them off at the post office.

A few minutes later he pulled into a parking spot of the post office while McKenzie pulled out some money before leaving her backpack on the seat. Once inside she paid the clerk, and he told them that Kate should get the package by ten o'clock the next morning.

"Hopefully, Kate can test the hairs and call us with the results later in the afternoon. And let's hope that's soon enough," McKenzie said as they walked back to the pickup.

The girls rode in silence as Derek drove to the feed store. McKenzie rolled down the window and let the warm air blow through her hair.

"Are you girls eager for the rodeo? I've watched you practice. You've both improved a lot since you came to Emma's." Derek tuned the radio to a country music station.

"McKenzie will win her category. She's really good. She finishes a lot faster than me," Bailey said as she folded her arms across her chest.

"Oh, I'm not that good," McKenzie said, turning to Bailey. "There are a lot of riders who are better than I am."

"I don't know about that," Bailey said dismally. "You'll still win, and I bet you win the Junior Miss Rodeo Queen contest, too."

McKenzie didn't know what to say to cheer Bailey up. She knew how badly her younger friend wanted to keep up with her. Though Bailey rode well, McKenzie knew she would have tough competition at the rodeo. Many of the competitors had their own horses and rode daily. Bailey didn't have her own horse and had few opportunities to ride.

"Hey, why don't you enter the sheep chase, Bailey?" Derek asked.

"That's a great idea," McKenzie said cheerfully. "I've done that before. It's a lot of fun, but I'm too old now."

"What's the sheep chase?" Bailey looked at McKenzie.

"Kids are turned loose in a pen of sheep. The first kid to catch a sheep and hold on to it is the winner. You could do that," McKenzie said with a smile.

"Sounds cool to me," Derek said as he pulled into the parking lot of the feed store. "How about it?"

"I don't know," Bailey said reluctantly. Then she continued, "I suppose I could try. It does sound like fun."

Derek parked at the loading dock beside a pickup with CEDAR CREEK RANCH printed across the door. He turned to the girls and handed McKenzie a few bills. "Go on in and grab a couple of drinks. My treat."

McKenzie hesitated and then thanked Derek. Within a couple of minutes, the girls returned with icy cold drinks.

"When are we going to tell Emma about the horse in the dugout?" Bailey said after Derek went inside the store.

"I don't know," McKenzie replied. "Now that she hurt her arm, I hate to give her something else to worry about."

Bailey nodded in agreement. "And we can't tell her we suspect Derek when we don't know for sure," she whispered.

Derek loaded the back of the pickup with feed. Then they headed back to Sunshine Stables. While Derek unloaded the pickup, the girls went to the house.

McKenzie dropped her backpack to the floor, and then the girls headed back outside to the stables. They needed to help the stable hands with the extra chores because Emma was gone.

The rest of the afternoon flew by in a blur and in the early evening, they went inside and found Mrs. Wilson cooking in the kitchen.

"I found a recipe for orange chicken and fried rice on the counter," Mrs. Wilson said cheerfully. "Emma must have been planning on fixing it for supper, so I decided to try it."

Bailey's eyes lit up. "My grandma from China sent the recipe to my mom. It's my favorite. I told Emma about it and she wanted to try it."

McKenzie was glad Mrs. Wilson was staying with them. She knew Bailey was worried about not doing well in the rodeo. Ever since Emma had gotten hurt, Bailey had been quieter, but having Mrs. Wilson in the house seemed to perk her up.

After supper the girls practiced barrel racing. McKenzie and Bailey timed each other. McKenzie gave Bailey a few pointers on tightening her turns around the barrels. Soon, she had improved her time by a couple of seconds.

After heading inside the house, McKenzie noticed the backpack she had dropped earlier. As she picked it up, she noticed the zipper was partially open. She was sure she had zipped it closed before going into the post office earlier in the day. Who would have opened it? As she flung the backpack onto her shoulder, she noticed a sheet of paper stuffed inside. She pulled it out and gasped.

A handwritten message read: "Tell no one about the mystery horse if you ever want to see it alive again."

At The Rodeo

"Who wrote this note and put it in my backpack?" McKenzie's hand trembled as she handed it to Bailey.

"Didn't you have it with you all the time we were in town?" Bailey asked.

McKenzie thought for a minute. "I left it in the pickup when I went to the hospital, the post office, and the feed store."

"Derek waited in the pickup while we went to the post office," Bailey said as she chewed on a fingernail.

McKenzie didn't answer. Derek was the only person who had been alone with the backpack. Had he written the note? Could he really be the thief after all?

More than anything, McKenzie wanted to talk to Emma. But that was out of the question now. The thief had threatened to kill the horse if they told anyone.

McKenzie was getting more scared by the minute. She needed time to think. She had to find some way to get help without Diamond Girl getting hurt. She clenched her eyes shut and prayed, asking God to help her and to keep the horse safe.

McKenzie was so concerned about the threatening note that she had little time to think about the Rodeo Queen contest tomorrow.

When she woke in the morning, worrisome thoughts filled her mind. She peered at Bailey, who was lying wide-awake on the bottom bunk.

"I can't believe the rodeo starts today," McKenzie said. "I am so nervous about the pageant. What if I mess up?"

"You won't, but I'll take your place if you want," Bailey said with a slight grin.

"Believe me, I'd let you if I could." McKenzie sat up and swung her legs over the side of the top bunk. "I'd rather be in the sheep chase with you."

"You're kidding," Bailey said. Then she added longingly. "I would give anything to be in the pageant."

McKenzie hopped from her bunk and pulled on a pair of jeans. After finishing chores, Derek planned to take the horses to the rodeo grounds. He would settle them into their stalls until Mrs. Wilson brought the girls in later. That way McKenzie would have plenty of time to get ready for the pageant.

Then, after the crowning of the Rodeo Queen and the Junior Miss Rodeo Queen, Bailey would take part in the kids' sheep chase. Following that, the girls would compete in the barrel-racing and calf-roping contests.

Finally, the girls finished the morning chores and helped Derek and Ian load their horses into the trailer. They watched as Derek pulled out of the driveway and disappeared down the road in a cloud of dust.

McKenzie glanced at her watch. "Kate should have received our package by now. I'm going to call her and see if she's found out anything about the hair yet."

She scrolled through the list of names in her cell phone and clicked on Kate's name. After a few rings, a familiar voice came on the line. McKenzie heard a dog bark in the background.

"Hi, Kate. Did you get the package?" McKenzie asked.

"I don't know. I haven't been home all morning. Mom made an appointment for Biscuit to get his shots. We won't be home till after lunch," Kate said.

McKenzie groaned. "This is really important. I have the feeling that guy will move the horse soon. We need to find out if the horse is Diamond Girl, so we can rescue her before she disappears again."

"Mom wants to stop at a sale at the shoe store, but I'll see if I can hurry her. I'll tell her it's important that we get home," Kate said.

"Thanks, Kate. Call me as soon as you get the results,

okay? And give Biscuit a hug from his Auntie McKenzie."
After saying good-bye, McKenzie flipped the phone shut
and filled Bailey in on the conversation.

After eating a quick lunch, the girls headed to their
bedroom. McKenzie pulled on her new black jeans and
the sparkly green blouse. Bailey looked longingly at
McKenzie as she helped apply her makeup. But a smile
twitched the corners of Bailey's mouth when McKenzie
asked her to french braid her hair.

As Bailey worked, McKenzie thought about the
contest. Her stomach churned at the thought of the
judging. She had an interview with the judges and then
she must ride her horse in a specific pattern before them.

"Are you girls about ready to go?" Mrs. Wilson
hollered up the stairs.

"Just finishing up," Bailey called through the open
door. Then she tied a green bow onto McKenzie's braid.
"There. We're done."

The girls grabbed their backpacks filled with a change
of clothes for the rodeo events. McKenzie grabbed the
threatening note and stuffed it into her jeans pocket. A
few minutes later, the girls tossed their bags and cowboy
hats into the back seat of Mrs. Wilson's car.

Mrs. Wilson told them that Emma would soon be
released from the hospital. The doctors had found no

sign of a concussion. Once she'd dropped the girls off at the rodeo, Mrs. Wilson would pick up her daughter.

The girls sighed with relief at the news. All too soon they pulled into the parking lot of the rodeo grounds. Mrs. Wilson stopped the car outside the building where the judges were waiting. McKenzie agreed to meet Bailey at the stalls after the interview, and then Mrs. Wilson and Bailey went on to the stables to find Derek and the horses.

McKenzie clutched her cowboy hat as she headed to the building where the judges held the interviews. She sat on a folding chair in the room with ten other girls. As she waited her turn, she glanced at the other competitors. She knew they were all probably wondering who would be crowned the next Junior Miss Rodeo Queen.

A young woman arrived carrying a clipboard and called McKenzie's name. After wiping her sweaty palms on her jeans, McKenzie followed the woman to a row of judges in the next room. They sat behind a table, staring at her. A white-haired woman with dark-rimmed glasses perched on the end of her nose asked her questions about her family and school. A chubby man with a black goatee asked her why she wanted to be crowned Junior Miss Rodeo Queen.

McKenzie managed to answer their questions,

though afterward she couldn't even remember what the questions were. She breathed a sigh of relief when she finished her interview and returned to her chair in the other room. When all the contestants had been interviewed, the woman with the clipboard returned. She told them to bring their horses to the show ring in ten minutes to begin the horsemanship contest.

Sahara had the same stall every year at the rodeo, so McKenzie knew where to find her. Derek, who had been at the rodeo grounds all day, was running a brush over the horse's backside when McKenzie arrived. Bailey was sitting cross-legged on the tack box and jumped to her feet when McKenzie approached.

"How'd you do?" Bailey asked.

McKenzie shrugged. "Not very good. I was nervous and talked too fast. I didn't know how to answer some of the questions. I really messed up."

Before Bailey could answer, Derek spoke up. "Let's get your horse over to the arena."

McKenzie waited her turn outside the arena, wondering if her parents and brother had arrived. She hoped Emma would get here in time to see the performance, too. As she listened to the announcer's voice over the loudspeaker, she watched the faces of the other girls as they finished their routines. Some of them beamed with pride, while others hung their heads in disappointment.

McKenzie mounted Sahara, scanning the crowd outside the arena, looking for her family. When she didn't see them, she turned to Bailey. "I think I'm going to be sick."

"You can't be sick now. The announcer just called your name," Bailey said.

McKenzie prepared to enter the arena but turned as a familiar voice called her name. Emma stood several feet away giving her a thumbs-up.

McKenzie beamed. She turned and rode into the arena. She took a deep breath and began her routine, trying to remember everything Emma had taught her. The judges expected her to keep her seat in the saddle and her hands in view the entire time, and of course, she must smile constantly.

As she finished her routine, she saluted the judges. They scribbled notes on pieces of paper. Though the judges smiled back, McKenzie couldn't tell what they thought of her performance. They probably smiled at everybody. She and the other contestants would have to wait awhile longer to learn who would be crowned queen.

McKenzie led Sahara back to the stables. As she watered her horse, she heard voices shouting. Turning, she saw her mom, dad, and little brother, Evan.

"McKenzie, you did a wonderful job!" Mrs. Phillips exclaimed.

After giving her family a round of hugs, McKenzie saw Emma and Bailey approaching. Everyone told McKenzie she had done well, but she knew she had made several small mistakes. Several contestants had performed perfectly. She wished she had done better, but she was also glad the contest was almost over. Now, she only had to wait.

McKenzie watched the remaining girls perform. After the contestants took their horses to their stalls, they all returned to the arena. McKenzie's palms grew sweaty as she climbed the steps of the stage at one end of the arena.

One by one, each of the girls walked across the stage to the microphone. Each girl introduced herself to the crowd then returned to her place in line.

McKenzie's heart fluttered wildly as she waited her turn. She closed her eyes and prayed, "Dear God, help me to not forget my name."

When she opened her eyes, the announcer, a middle-aged man with graying hair, was staring at her. The girl next to her nudged her with her elbow. McKenzie's legs felt rubbery as she walked to the microphone. She took a deep breath and smiled at the crowd.

A voice she didn't recognize came out her mouth. "Hi. I'm McKenzie Phillips. My parents are Dan and Jen Phillips, and I have a little brother, Evan, who is eight years old. I will be an eighth grader this fall at White Sulfur Springs Junior High."

The crowd clapped as she returned to her place in line. She felt the butterflies in her stomach settle down as she listened to the other girls' introductions.

"Well, there you have it, folks. Let's give all of these lovely young ladies a round of applause," the announcer exclaimed.

When the applause died down, he continued. "Our judges had quite a time choosing a winner. In a few minutes we'll crown our new Junior Miss Rodeo Queen. But first let's hear it for our second runner-up—Amanda Bradford!"

McKenzie clapped for the tall black-haired girl next to her. She knew she didn't stand a chance of being crowned queen, but secretly she had wished to be a runner-up. She held her breath as the announcer continued.

"Our first runner-up is—Taylor McCowen!" The announcer's voice boomed above the cheering crowd.

As McKenzie's gaze darted over the audience,

she wondered who would be crowned queen. She thought about the brown-haired girl on the end. Her performance had looked almost perfect, and she had the confidence of a much older girl.

McKenzie barely heard the announcer as he continued. "And now is the moment we've all been waiting for. Our new Junior Miss Rodeo Queen is. . . McKenzie Phillips!"

McKenzie heard the cheering crowd as she forced herself to center stage. Her knees wobbled as a young woman placed a sparkly crown over her black cowboy hat and pinned a sash across her green blouse.

For a minute, McKenzie forgot the duties of the Junior Miss Rodeo Queen, then she remembered and walked to the front of the stage. As cameras flashed, she waved to the crowd.

Before she knew it, she was whisked off stage. Soon her family, Emma, and Bailey surrounded her. Everyone talked at once, hugging and congratulating her.

Bailey stood to the back and finally came forward sheepishly. "You did great, McKenzie. I guess if I couldn't win, I'm glad you did."

McKenzie felt better knowing that Bailey was okay with her winning. Later she would let Bailey wear the crown.

After a photographer took her picture for the

newspaper, the woman with the clipboard walked up to her. "We need to get you and your horse over to the arena. It's time for the rodeo to start."

McKenzie knew that the Junior Miss Rodeo Queen got to carry the Montana state flag around the arena, while the Rodeo Queen carried the American flag.

Moments later she settled onto Sahara's back, gripping the flagpole tightly in her hands. As "The Star Spangled Banner" boomed over the loudspeaker, the two flag bearers galloped around the arena. When the anthem ended, they stopped in the center of the ring while the crowd stood and cheered. Seconds later the girls rode their horses out of the ring.

After returning Sahara to her stall, McKenzie hurried back to the arena. The air was filled with the wonderful smells of rodeo foods—onion rings, hot dogs, cotton candy. She approached the fence to watch Bailey in the first rodeo event—the sheep chase. McKenzie said a silent prayer. She asked God to help Bailey do her best.

Some workers sectioned off an end of the arena and then several sheep were herded into the ring. All the kids competing in the sheep chase stood at one end and waited. When the starting pistol cracked, they all darted forward, trying to catch one of the woolly animals.

"Go, Bailey!" McKenzie cheered.

The kids raced after the sheep that were scurrying in all directions. One boy had a sheep by the hind leg, but then it squirmed out of his grasp. Bailey ran and fell as she cornered a sheep. As she scrambled to her feet, another sheep ran by her. She reached out and grabbed a hind leg, but the sheep was stronger. It pulled her across the ground. She held on tightly. As the sheep tried to run on three legs, Bailey reached out and grabbed the other hind leg.

The sheep struggled, but Bailey held on. She clutched the sheep until a worker clapped her on the shoulder. Bailey had won!

"Way to go, Bailey!" McKenzie shouted above the roaring crowd.

As the Junior Miss Rodeo Queen, McKenzie had the honor of presenting Bailey with her first-place blue ribbon. The younger girl beamed with pride as she followed McKenzie out of the arena.

McKenzie had little time to talk with Bailey. The younger riders in the barrel-racing contest would soon warm up. Bailey stuffed her blue ribbon in her back pocket and headed to the gate where Derek held Applejack's reins.

Soon Bailey and the first riders galloped into the arena, warming up for the competition. Bailey sat stiffly on Applejack's back, riding faster than her competitors.

McKenzie watched from behind the fence. She heard the bulls snort in their pens as they waited for the bull-riding competition. A rodeo clown wearing huge polka-dotted pants and a big, red nose teased some kids in the first row of bleachers. A toddler grabbed at his orange wig, nearly pulling it off.

As McKenzie watched the clown, a crash sounded from the bull pens. The crowd shrieked. Turning back to the arena, she gasped. A huge white bull had broken out of its pen. The frightened young riders on their horses scattered about the arena.

McKenzie saw Bailey glance at the raging bull behind her. Terror filled Bailey's dark eyes as she dug her heels into Applejack's side. She flicked the reins, urging the horse to run faster.

McKenzie screamed when Bailey lost her balance and tumbled from her horse. The wild bull pawed at the ground, flinging dirt behind him. He put his head down and snorted. With his black eyes on Bailey, the bull lunged!

The Escape

Bailey screamed. The clown jumped over the fence and waved a red flag. The bull turned and pawed the ground before charging after him. The clown jumped out of the way, teasing the bull to lure it away from Bailey.

A young rodeo worker darted into the ring. He swept Bailey into his arms and lifted her over the fence to safety. Several men jumped in the ring and guided the angry bull back into his pen.

The audience cheered. McKenzie began to relax when she saw Bailey safely standing beside Applejack. Thankfully, Bailey would have time to recover from her scare before her turn came.

Finally the announcer called Bailey's name, and she rode into the arena. She flicked the reins, dug her heels into her horse's sides, and darted across the starting line. She raced toward the first barrel, turning a wide circle around it.

She urged Applejack faster as she headed toward

the second barrel, but had trouble slowing down for the turn. Bailey made a near perfect turn on the third barrel and raced for the finish line.

"Your turn is coming soon, young lady." McKenzie heard a man beside her speak.

Turning, she saw Derek. "I was hoping to hear the results first. I sure hope Bailey places at least third."

"It could be a close race. There was a lot of tough competition in her group. You'd better bring Sahara to the gate. It's almost time." Derek hurried away to help Bailey lead Applejack back to the stall.

As McKenzie hurried to Sahara's stall, she heard the announcer give the results. She sighed when Bailey's name wasn't called. She hoped her friend wasn't too disappointed.

"Hey, Ian. Thanks," McKenzie said as she saw Emma's stable hand leading Sahara out of the stables.

"Go get 'em," Ian said, giving McKenzie a high five.

McKenzie grabbed the reins and headed back to the arena. Only three more riders before it was her turn. Her stomach quivered, but it wasn't like being on stage for the queen contest. She loved this kind of competition.

Finally McKenzie rode into the arena. She dug in her heels and lunged forward with Sahara. She turned the first two turns tightly around the barrels, but the third was slow and wide. On the final stretch to the finish line, she urged Sahara faster.

Her time was her best yet, but she didn't know if it was good enough to win. Several more riders had to compete.

Bailey was waiting for McKenzie in the stables when she returned with Sahara. "I've got news!"

"What?" McKenzie asked as she tied her horse in her stall.

Bailey glanced around to make sure no one was near. "The guy we've seen riding the spotted horse is here."

McKenzie stared at Bailey. "Do you know where he is now?"

Bailey glanced about the crowd and grabbed McKenzie's arm. "There he is—standing by the fence next to the grandstand. He's wearing the black cowboy hat."

As McKenzie watched, he turned and looked right at her. She turned away, and when she glanced back, he had vanished.

"He saw me looking at him. Now he's gone," she whispered.

Bailey edged closer to McKenzie. "I've been thinking. Shouldn't we have heard from Kate by now?"

McKenzie pulled her cell phone from her pocket. "I turned it off and forgot to turn it back on."

She listened to her voice mail. "Hi, McKenzie. This is Kate. Give me a call as soon as you can. I'll be home all evening. Bye."

As soon as she flipped her phone shut, the crowd around her cheered. McKenzie turned to see the last rider in her division compete. She wondered where she stood in the rankings.

The announcer's voice boomed over the loudspeaker. "That's it for the girls' barrel-riding competition. I've never seen a closer race, folks. But the young lady with the fastest time is McKenzie Phillips from White Sulfur Springs!"

McKenzie felt as if her heart would leap from her chest. She didn't even hear who came in second and third place. Bailey jumped up and down and clutched McKenzie's arm.

McKenzie felt dazed as she stepped into the arena. The crowd cheered as the Senior Rodeo Queen handed her a trophy. She had worked hard for it, but she knew she couldn't have won it without God's help.

When she stepped out of the arena, Bailey met her. The younger girl's eyes flashed with excitement.

"Wow, is that ever cool!" Bailey said as McKenzie held the trophy for her to see. "I sure hope I get one someday."

"You've still got a chance today. The calf-roping contest will start in about an hour," McKenzie said as she glanced at her watch.

McKenzie turned to her parents and Evan, who had come up behind her. Mrs. Phillips handed McKenzie a set of keys. "Why don't you lock your trophy up in the pickup? We parked on the side street behind the stables. Then you girls can meet us at Hamburger Haven before your next event."

McKenzie took the keys and turned to Bailey, "Let's call Kate when we get to the pickup and have some privacy."

The two girls headed across the rodeo grounds and past the horse stables. Cars and pickups lined the side street while dozens of horse trailers were parked in a shaded lot beside the street.

"Hey, look!" Bailey grabbed McKenzie's arm and pointed at a man carrying a bucket of water across the lot. "There's the mystery man. I wonder why he's carrying water out here."

Dusk was settling in and McKenzie squinted at the figure walking through the shadows. "He's heading toward Maggie's pickup and trailer. Maybe he works for her. He must be carrying water to Frisco."

"Why wouldn't she be in the stables with the other horses?" Bailey asked.

"I don't know," McKenzie answered. "Maybe he's tied her in those trees behind the trailer."

The girls stopped when they reached the Phillips' pickup. McKenzie slid onto the backseat and pulled out her cell phone. She clicked on Kate's name and waited while the phone dialed the number.

"Hi, Kate. What did you find out?" McKenzie blurted when Kate answered.

"I didn't think you were ever going to call. There's no doubt about it. I tested the hairs you sent me," Kate said excitedly. "I can't prove they came from Diamond Girl, but the hairs have definitely been dyed."

"You're positive?" McKenzie asked as her excitement mounted.

"I'm 100 percent sure," Kate said. "Let me know if I can do anything else."

"Would you let the other Camp Club Girls know what is going on? We need all the prayers we can get."

Kate agreed and McKenzie snapped the phone shut. The girls headed back to the rodeo grounds. "We need to call Emma and tell her everything. We know the man who rode the spotted horse is here at the rodeo, so it would be a perfect time for Emma to go to Old Towne and check out the horse. She'll know if it's Diamond Girl with a dye job."

McKenzie put in a call to Emma, but she didn't answer. "Maybe she can't hear her phone with all the noise of the rodeo."

As they approached Hamburger Haven, McKenzie saw her family. "What took you girls so long? You barely have time to eat now before the calf roping starts." Mrs. Phillips handed them each a sandwich. "You'd better get Sahara ready. We'll be watching you."

McKenzie shoved the last bite of hamburger into her mouth as they stepped into the stable. She stuffed the napkin into her pocket. The stable buzzed with voices and neighing as riders prepared their horses for competitions.

"Hey, McKenzie." Bailey grabbed McKenzie's arm. "There's Frisco's stall."

McKenzie stared at the name above the stall. It read: MAGGIE PRESTON—FRISCO. McKenzie looked at the black mustang. She thought about the man carrying the bucket to the trailer. Something didn't make sense. Why was he carrying water there, when Maggie's horse was in the stable?

Suddenly McKenzie had an idea. She saw Maggie approach the stall. "Hey, Maggie, would you write down the names of those riders we watched roping calves at your stable? I want to watch them compete."

Maggie looked skeptically at the girls as she took a bite of her candy bar. *Where else have I seen that candy bar wrapper?* McKenzie thought. Maggie grabbed a pen and wrote on the napkin McKenzie gave her.

"McKenzie and Bailey, line up!" a voice called. McKenzie looked up as Derek led Sahara up the aisle toward them.

McKenzie thanked Maggie and stuffed the napkin back into her pocket. She took Sahara's reins from Derek. They arrived at the arena gate as the announcer was calling their names.

McKenzie had no time to get nervous. She grabbed her lasso in one hand and mounted Sahara. Bailey climbed on behind her.

The moment the calf came out of the chute, McKenzie darted after it. The calf kicked as it ran, but McKenzie focused and as it lifted its head, she tossed the lasso. The loop sailed through the air and landed around the calf's neck. Keeping a firm grip on the lasso, McKenzie slid from Sahara's back.

She raced to the calf with Bailey close behind her. Together, the girls wrapped the other end of the rope around the calf's legs so it couldn't run away.

McKenzie had no idea whether their time was good compared to the other competitors. Right now, her thoughts were on Diamond Girl. Winning the calf-roping competition was the last thing on her mind.

They rode out of the arena while McKenzie glanced at the horses and riders lining up for the women's barrel-racing competition. Darkness had settled over the crowd, but the overhead pole lights had come on. She stopped beneath a light near a hitching post and pulled the crumpled napkin and the threatening note from her pocket.

"Look, Bailey. The handwriting is identical," McKenzie whispered to Bailey. "Maggie's pickup was in the parking lot of the feed store yesterday."

Bailey gasped. "You mean Maggie wrote both notes? So that's why you asked Maggie to write down those names."

McKenzie nodded. "Remember that candy bar Maggie was eating? That's the kind of candy wrapper that was in the dugout."

McKenzie glanced around her. Maggie stood in line for the barrel racing, adjusting Frisco's saddle. A man in a black jacket and cowboy hat stood beside her.

McKenzie gasped. He was the man who had ridden the spotted horse. As he turned away from her, McKenzie saw the red lettering on the back of his jacket: WHISPERING PINES HORSE THERAPY RANCH.

"Oh, Bailey," she whispered. "We've got trouble. Big trouble!"

The announcer's voice boomed over the loudspeaker, interrupting the girls' conversation. "The third-place trophy in the girls' calf-roping contest goes to McKenzie Phillips and Bailey Chang."

McKenzie quickly slid from Sahara's back and looped the reins around the hitching post. Bailey's eyes gleamed as the girls hurried into the arena. Bailey's hands trembled as she accepted her trophy.

The girls hurried out of the arena, not even waiting to hear the first-and second-place winners. McKenzie whispered in Bailey's ear. "Let's get out of here. We have to get back to the trailer lot. Quickly! I know a shortcut." She nodded toward a narrow street beyond the stables.

"What's going on?"

"I think I know where Diamond Girl is," McKenzie said. "We have to hurry to rescue her. But we can't look obvious. As soon as Maggie races with Frisco, she'll head out of here, taking Diamond Girl with her."

The girls quietly rode Sahara through the stable area to the back street. They could hardly hear the loud voices of the crowd and blaring music of the rodeo.

Hurrying beneath the dim streetlights, they arrived at Maggie's trailer and pickup. McKenzie slid off Sahara's back and peeked inside the trailer.

"She's not here," McKenzie whispered. "She can't be far. Wait here. Tell me if anyone comes."

McKenzie set off for the grove of trees, keeping to the shadows and calling, "Hey, girl, are you here?"

A soft whinny came from inside the grove. McKenzie pushed through the brambles. Soon she saw the white spots on the horse, barely visible in the darkness.

As she touched the horse, Bailey's cry reached her.

"Someone's coming, McKenzie. Run!"

McKenzie quickly untied the horse's reins and led her out of the trees. "Go get Derek," she cried to Bailey.

She jumped on the horse's back and dug in her heels. McKenzie knew the spotted horse was Diamond Girl. She had to get her to safety. She raced the horse as fast as she dared. She heard hooves thunder behind her. She turned. In the moonlight she glimpsed the strange man chasing her on Frisco!

He screamed at her to stop. She dug in her heels, urging Diamond Girl to run faster. "Dear God, please help us," McKenzie prayed.

Where could she hide? She couldn't run forever. The hooves continued to pound the ground behind her. More voices shouted at her to stop. Glancing behind her, she saw two more figures on horses approaching. It was too dark to recognize them. She urged Diamond Girl onward. Soon the thundering hooves began to fade. She was losing at least two of them.

Suddenly, a horse came from the darkness behind her. "McKenzie," a voice cried out. It was Derek, riding Sahara. McKenzie pulled Diamond Girl to a walk.

"Ian stopped the guy who was chasing you. We've called security. You're safe and so is Diamond Girl," Derek said. "Bailey told us about her. But who did this to her?"

McKenzie brought Diamond Girl to a halt.

"It's Maggie," she said frantically. "Maggie stole Diamond Girl to use at a horse therapy farm. We have to stop her before she gets away."

Derek stared at her, and then snapped the reins. "Let's go!"

McKenzie and Derek spun their horses around. They raced back to the lot where McKenzie's family and Emma had gathered.

Maggie's accomplice had broken free from Ian. He'd already loaded Frisco into the trailer. Maggie was behind the wheel, trying to move the pickup out of a tight parking spot.

"Don't let them go!" McKenzie screamed. "They're the horse thieves."

Mr. Phillips looked at his daughter and jumped into

his pickup. Seconds later he had parked in the roadway, blocking Maggie in. The rodeo security guards arrived at the scene, ordering Maggie and her accomplice to get out of the pickup.

McKenzie hopped off Diamond Girl and led her to Bailey, Emma, and her family. Minutes later, McKenzie saw the flashing red and blue lights of the sheriff's pickup. A police car followed. The sheriff listened to the girls' story. After talking with Maggie and her friend, he ordered them into the police car.

Questions came to McKenzie from different directions. She and Bailey quickly explained everything.

First, they told about finding the spotted horse at Old Towne. They explained about snipping the hairs and sending them to Kate. When the girls saw Frisco in her stall at the rodeo, McKenzie knew the strange man carrying water to the trailer lot must have a horse hidden somewhere. She had come to suspect Maggie when she saw the moving boxes at Cedar Creek, so McKenzie had asked her to write down the riders' names so she could compare the handwriting. Then McKenzie remembered where she had seen Maggie's candy bar before. *The same kind of wrapper was in the trash at the dugout!* McKenzie thought.

Then, when she saw WHISPERING PINES HORSE

THERAPY RANCH on the stranger's jacket, she realized the truth. Maggie and her friend, whose name was Chuck Hanson, had stolen Diamond Girl for their new therapy ranch.

The sheriff commended the girls on their hard work. Maggie and Chuck had confessed to everything. Maggie admitted that with Diamond Girl out of the rodeo competition, Frisco was a sure winner. She had planned to leave with Diamond Girl while Sunshine Stables staff was preoccupied at the rodeo, not only with a prize-winning racehorse, but also a splendid therapy horse to draw customers to her new ranch.

Mr. Phillips came to his daughter's side as McKenzie watched Derek and Ian load the horses into the trailer.

"Dad, you were right when you said that guilt is God telling us something." McKenzie looked up at her father. "I suspected an innocent person of a crime. I don't feel very good about it."

Mr. Phillips put an arm around his daughter's shoulder. "Sometimes we have to forgive ourselves just like God forgives us."

McKenzie thought about that as the sheriff drove away with Maggie and Chuck. Though she knew she would get over her anger at them, she still felt sorry for them and wondered what would happen to them next.

"You girls were amazing!" Emma's eyes lit up for the first time all week. "Thanks to you, Sunshine Stables will soon be back to normal!"

"You were right when you said everything happens for a reason," McKenzie said. "God had a purpose for bringing Diamond Girl back to you tonight."

Emma looked quizzically at McKenzie, "And what would that be?"

"There are more barrel-riding competitions tomorrow night. You never withdrew after Diamond Girl disappeared. Why don't you race her one more time? That is, if you feel like it."

Diamond Girl whinnied from inside the trailer. Emma laughed. "You know, McKenzie. By tomorrow, I may feel pretty well. I just might do that."

If you enjoyed

McKENZIE'S MONTANA MYSTERY

be sure to read other

CAMP CLUB GIRLS

books from BARBOUR PUBLISHING

Book 1: Mystery at Discovery Lake

ISBN 978-1-60260-267-0

Book 2: Sydney's DC Discovery

ISBN 978-1-60260-268-7

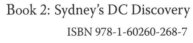

Book 4: Alexis and the Sacramento Surprise

ISBN 978-1-60260-270-0

Book 5: Kate's Philadelphia Frenzy

ISBN 978-1-60260-271-7

Book 6: Bailey's Peoria Problem

ISBN 978-1-60260-272-4

AVAILABLE WHEREVER BOOKS ARE SOLD.